Neil Si

45 Seconds from Broadway

A SAMUEL FRENCH ACTING EDITION

New York Hollywood London Toronto

SAMUELFRENCH.COM

ISBN 978-0-573-62850-4 Printed in U.S.A. #24

IMPORTANT BILLING AND CREDIT REQUIREMENTS

All producers of 45 SECONDS FROM BROADWAY *must* give credit to the Author of the Play in all programs distributed in connection with performances of the Play and in all instances in which the title of the Play appears for purposes of advertising, publicizing or otherwise exploiting the Play and/or a production. The name of the Author *must* also appear on a separate line, on which no other name appears, immediately following the title, and *must* appear in size of type not less than fifty percent the size of the title type.

Billing *must* substantially be as follows:

(NAME OF PRODUCER)
presents

45 SECONDS FROM BROADWAY

by

Neil Simon

RICHARD RODGERS THEATRE

UNDER THE DIRECTION OF THE MESSRS. NEDERLANDER

Emanuel Azenberg Ira Pittelman
James Nederlander Scott Nederlander Kevin McCollum

present

Neil Simon's
45 Seconds From Broadway

Starring

Lewis J. Stadlen

Louis Zorich Rebecca Schull

with

David Margulies
Lynda Gravátt

Kevin Carroll Dennis Creaghan Julie Lund Bill Moor
and
Judith Blazer Alix Korey

also starring

Marian Seldes

Scenic Design
John Lee Beatty

Costume Design
William Ivey Long

Lighting Design
Paul Gallo

Sound Design
Peter J. Fitzgerald

Special Effects
Gregory Meeh

Wig and Hair Design
Paul Huntley

Technical Supervision
Brian Lynch
Neil A. Mazzella

Production Supervisor
Steven Beckler

Casting by
Jay Binder, C.S.A.

Media Advisor
Alan Bernhard

Press Representative
Bill Evans & Associates

Associate Producer
Ginger Montel

General Manager
Abbie M. Strassler

Directed by

Jerry Zaks

ACT I

(We are in the coffee shop/restaurant off the lobby of a mid-priced, second rate hotel in the Broadway Theatre District of New York.

There are ten to twelve tables squeezed into the dining area. The tables have dark wood and chairs, no tablecloths, but paper napkins.

A door at stage right is the entrance from the street. Another door at stage left is the door that comes in and goes out to the lobby of the hotel.

On the back wall are dozens of photos of young actors, all signed and no one you ever heard of.

At the rear wall, behind a small counter, are the doors that lead in and out of the kitchen.)

Scene 1
"Summer"

(AT RISE: About eleven thirty in the morning. We hear a clap of thunder and the sound of rain against the street window.

The restaurant is virtually empty except for two men, each seated on opposite sides of the room

One is well-dressed, early fifties, sitting near the window, the preferred spot for the regulars. He is looking at a well-worn menu through his horned-rimmed glasses. His name is ANDREW DUNCAN and he is British.

The man on the other side is African. He is wearing a worn-out jacket and a shirt that could use ironing. He eats soup hungrily from a large bowl, breaking off pieces of bread and mixing them in his soup. He also has a cup of coffee.

Suddenly the street door opens and a man rushes in, partly wet from the rain. He holds an umbrella that has blown inside out with the struts pointing straight out.

This is MICKEY FOX, about sixty, vigorous and alert. He is a Jewish comedian and makes no attempt to hide the accent he grew up with in the lower East Side of New York.)

MICKEY. *(To no one.)* Goddamn umbrella! Judy Garland flew in from Kansas with dis ting. *(He sees ANDREW.)* How are you?

ANDREW. *(Stands, smiles.)* Hello. Fine, thank you. Good to see you.

(MICKEY looks at the MAN eating the soup.)

MICKEY. Hi. *(The MAN gives half a nod, then goes back to his soup. To ANDREW.)* If I got one guess to pick the producer who flew in from London to meet me, I pick you.

ANDREW. *(Smiles.)* Yes. Andrew Duncan.

MICKEY. Excuse me, Andrew. *(He turns to the MAN eating soup.)* Nothing poisonal, mind you, but you look like someone who never hoid of me.... These things are possible.... Mickey Fox, I'm playing in the theater next door.... You don't know what I'm talking about.... I don't blame you.... I see a man sitting alone, I want to say hello.... I don't know where I'm going with dis.... *(He takes out a personal card.)* Here's my card.... Show dis at the box office, you'll get in for half price.... Okay?

(He turns back to ANDREW.)

ANDREW. *(As they shake.)* I just want to say it's a great—

MICKEY. *(Holds up his hand, back to SOLOMAN.)* Give me the card. *(SOLOMAN gives it to him. MICKEY tears it up.)* It's my second year, *everyone* gets in for half price.... *(He tears the card in half again, gives him the stub.)* ... Here. Show him dis, you'll get in for eight dollars.... *(He grabs the stub back.)* Forget it.... Just tell six people on the street you love Mickey Fox, you'll get in free and get a box of chocolate covered raisins.... We'll do this again sometime.... *(He turns back to ANDREW.)* Where were we?

ANDREW. I just want to say it's a great, *great* pleasure to meet you, Mr. Fox.

MICKEY. Please call me Mickey.... Not that it's my real name.... No one in my family has a real name.... They changed everything in Ellis Island.... I have an uncle named "NEXT!" I have an aunt named "OVER HERE, PLEASE."... My great grandfather was named "HOW MANY KIDS?" ... which later got changed to "HOWIE MANKITTS." ...

ANDREW. Well, in England we all know who Mickey Fox is.... May I say, I think you're one of the funniest men I've seen in my life.

MICKEY. Why? Who was the other one?... Oh, before we go any foither, Andrew, I think you should know they don't soive your kind of food here. English food.... They don't make twiffles here.

ANDREW. I don't think we have twiffles in England. Are you thinking of trifle? Trifle is a dessert.

MICKEY. I hoid of it, I never ate it. It never sounded good enough. I don't want a trifle. I want a *substantial*. Please, finish chewing your teabag.

ANDREW. *(Laughs again.)* I'm sorry, but you absolutely kill me.

MICKEY. Well, maybe later. We'll see how it goes.... I understand you're here to see my show tonight. You're my guest, of course.

ANDREW. Oh, I've already arranged for my seats, thank you.

MICKEY. You paid? Dat's nonsense.... *But* I don't want to insult you.... By the way, do you have any kids?

ANDREW. Yes. A boy.

MICKEY. *(Hands ANDREW the broken umbrella.)* A gift. From me to him.

ANDREW. *(Laughs, takes it.)* Thank you.

MICKEY. I know what you're thinking, "He's a little crazy," right? I've said it myself. Because a sane man wouldn't do my line of woik.... You noticed I said "woik." ... I can say it correctly ... work....

But which is funnier? Work ... or woik? I rest my case.

ANDREW. *(Laughs again.)* Indeed you do.

MICKEY. So, what's dis offer you have for me in London? *(ANDREW laughs.)* You laugh at that too? It was just a regular question.

ANDREW. I know. It's your timing. The way you say things. You can't help but be funny.

MICKEY. Thank you.... I can help it but it just don't pay as much.... So tell me what you have in mind for London?

ANDREW. Well, what my partners and I have been thinking about—

MICKEY. Before you continue, I hate to interrupt, especially a good English accent, I have a question.... Do you have any idea where you're sitting right now?

ANDREW. Were I'm sitting?... In a coffee shop on 46th Street.

MICKEY. Wrong.

ANDREW. 45th Street?

MICKEY. Wrong.

ANDREW. 47th?... I'm sorry. I don't know exactly.

MICKEY. Wrong!... Whatever you say is wrong.... If you said it *right* you would be wrong because you couldn't possibly know.... But I like you so I'll tell you.... You are sitting in the last bastion of what used to be the greatness of the Broadway Theater.

ANDREW. Really? Why is that?

MICKEY. Because you and I are here talking about a show. No one sits in coffee shops anymore talking about a show.... They talk about a moiger, a conglomerate, a buyout, a take out, a move out, a push over but not about a show.... But you'll see producers and theater owners with a billion dollars worth of theaters come in here for lunch and you know why?... Because it's cheap.... You see those pictures on the wall?... All young actors and actresses who you will never hear about in your life.... Because the owners, Bernie and Zelda, will say, "Stars don't need help. These kids need our help." ... And when dis place is gone, the entire Broadway will slide into the East River.

ANDREW. That's very sad, isn't it?

MICKEY. And it's coming.... A company like Yahoo Cisco Micro will come in and moige with Time Warner Kellogg's Raisin Corn Flakes and just like dat, no one will dot come in here anymore, right Bernie?

(BERNIE, the owner, crosses out of the kitchen and goes opposite to the cash register.)

BERNIE. Right.

MICKEY. But dis is no ordinary coffee shop.... There's one across the street, you get maybe scrambled eggs and an English looking muffin and dats it.... In here you get pot roast, potato pancakes, brisket, chicken livers, you understand? That's why people call this the Polish Tea Room.... And dats why important people like you and me eat here and not in some fancy, overpriced restaurant in Soho-hoho ... or in Tribeca, Try Shirley, Try Miriam.... You hear what I'm saying?

ANDREW. Perfectly.

MICKEY. Now tell me about the show in London and remember, I get twenty percent of the gross and I keep my wardrobe, even if we're doing "Camelot."

(MICKEY sits back, ANDREW leans in to talk business.
BERNIE crosses to the table where the MAN is finishing his soup.
BERNIE, in his early seventies, stands straight and looks as strong as an ox. He has a full head of gray/white hair. He's a charmer when he wants to be but don't fool with BERNIE. He can handle himself. The MAN, finishing his coffee, watches BERNIE put a slice of cake on his plate.)

BERNIE. Will that be all?

MAN. *(He speaks softly with the sound of Africa in it. It's an educated voice. He is polite but not bowed despite his worn clothing.)* What is this?

BERNIE. *(Writing out check.)* Pound cake. Just baked. Still warm.... Enjoy.

(He puts down the check, about to walk away.)

MAN. I didn't ask for cake.
BERNIE. There's no charge. With my compliments.
MAN. Do you give this to all your customers?
BERNIE. No. Just when I feel like.

(BERNIE starts for the register.)

MAN. If it's a gift, I don't have anything to give you in return.
BERNIE. *(Stops.)* Did I ask you? If you don't want it, leave it there.
MAN. I would like it very much. Thank you.

(He breaks it in half, puts half in a napkin in his pocket, and eats the other half.
BERNIE has crossed to the register to look at the day's bills and receipts.)

ANDREW. ... So it's not exactly your "One Man Show" we're talking about. After all, you've done your show in London many times and it's always, I might add, enormously successful.
MICKEY. Not true. I was not successful ....
ANDREW. Oh, come now. You did sellout business.
MICKEY. I take an oath on my life, I was not successful in London.... What I *was*, was da *biggest hit* dat country ever saw.... Some nights even *I* couldn't get in.... I say this in all humility, I was bigger than the Queen.... No disrespect. She's funny but her timing's a little slow.... *(ANDREW laughs. MICKEY grabs his hand.)* Stop laughing and listen.... Her trouble is, she speaks too English for the English.... People in da crowd are saying to each other, "What'd she say? Can you understand her? Who's the bald guy behind her?" She needs better representation.... So what have you got for me dat's better?

(The MAN gets up from his table and crosses to the register. He takes some money from his coat pocket, looks at it and looks at the

check.)

MAN. The bill is four dollars and eighty cents.... I have two dollars and ten cents. *(He shows it to BERNIE.)* I am not a vagrant nor a beggar. I will do whatever work you ask to repay you.

BERNIE. *(Looks at him, sighs softly.)* When you ordered, did you know you didn't have enough money?

MAN. Oh, yes. This is New York. I knew that two dollars and ten cents would not buy me much. But I was hungry. Please tell me what you want me to do.

(BERNIE's been through this before.)

BERNIE. What's your name, please?

MAN. For the police?

BERNIE. For me. What is it?

MAN. Soloman. Soloman Mantutu.

BERNIE. You're not from this country, are you?

SOLOMAN. From South Africa.... You are also not from this country, am I right?

BERNIE. Yes, but that doesn't make us related. *(The phone rings, BERNIE answers it.)* Hello?... How are you feeling?... *(He covers the phone, then to SOLOMAN.)* It's my wife. Will you please sit over there for a minute? *(SOLOMAN looks at chair, then sits, looks away from BERNIE.)* But you still have a fever, yes?... Zelda, there's no point coming down. It's raining.... It's a slow day. Very slow.

(He turns his back to SOLOMAN, continues into phone.)

ANDREW. *(To MICKEY.)* Are you available in September?

MICKEY. September? September?... No. I'm booked in September.

ANDREW. What about July?

MICKEY. In July I'm definitely booked.

ANDREW. I understand.... What about December?

MICKEY. Booked.

ANDREW. January?

MICKEY. Booked.... February, booked.... I'm always booked. I'm booked until I die ... and then I'm semi-booked....

(BERNIE hangs up the phone, looks at SOLOMAN.)

BERNIE. What kind of work did you do?

SOLOMAN. In South Africa? I was a teacher.

BERNIE. Is that why you came here? To teach?

SOLOMAN. No. I'm also a writer. I was brought to New York to put on my play. Unfortunately they could not raise enough money, not even to pay my way home. I'm learning very quickly how the American theater works.... Please tell me what you want me to do. I wish to go home as quickly as possible.

BERNIE. Alright. Go home. You don't owe me anything. That's a better deal than you got from your producers.... Gay gezint. It means good luck. *(He nods respectfully.)* Goodbye, Mr. Soloman.

(BERNIE picks up phone to dial.)

SOLOMAN. Not until I pay back my debt.

BERNIE. Soloman, I'm not going to starve without your four dollars and eighty cents. You have to get your plane fare somewhere else. Then go home and write a play they'll like in Africa.

(BERNIE looks at receipts.)

SOLOMAN. I've waited on tables before.

BERNIE. Oh, I see. You owe me money so now you want me to hire you as a waiter. So if you brought your family in for lunch and couldn't pay, I'd have to make you a partner.

SOLOMAN. You take your argument to a greater extreme than is necessary.

BERNIE. Oy, gut. I can already see the kind of plays you write. Goodbye again, Mr. Soloman.

SOLOMAN. *(Shows BERNIE the watch on his wrist.)* I would

give you my watch but it is broken beyond repair.

BERNIE. You know what your problem is, Soloman? You've got too much pride. Why can't you accept that I bought you lunch and in return, you gave me a valuable lesson in African logic?

SOLOMAN. Would you just take a minute and listen to my offer?

BERNIE. Your OFFER??... Soloman, I would like you to leave now.... Because if I get upset, I'll charge you for the cake.... And if I charge you for the cake, you'll wipe out my life savings.... Goodbye.

(BERNIE walks away. SOLOMAN watches him go, then turns and leaves through the door that leads to the hotel.)

MICKEY. *(Looking at menu, then to ANDREW.)* Listen Andrew. I know you invited me to lunch, but do you mind if I actually *eat* something?

ANDREW. By all means. Tell me what's good.

(ANDREW looks at the menu.)

MICKEY. Well, for what's good, you have to go somewhere else. But for what mother used to make, dis is da place.... I'm not talking about *your* mother. Your mother threw potatoes, watercress and chocolate biscuits into a pot, cooked it for eight seconds, and if it tasted lousy, she served it....

(ANDREW laughs heartily. They both look at their menus.
A young, pretty GIRL enters from the lobby door. Early twenties, carrying a shoulder purse and looking pretty nervous.... She stands there as if waiting for someone to help her. BERNIE sees her, crosses to her.)

BERNIE. You want to sit or are you waiting for someone?

MEGAN. I'm looking for a man named Bernie.

BERNIE. Bernie? That's me.... What can I do for you?

MEGAN. Anything would help. *(She takes a deep breath, lets it out.)* My name is Megan. Megan Woods?… I flew in from Ohio this morning and the airline lost one of my suitcases. The good one. They're still looking for it…. And I went to check into the hotel here but they can't find my reservation. It's a very small room but they still can't find it, my reservation, and the room I booked is already booked and it's nerve-racking enough to come to New York alone for the first time in your life and have all this happen. You know?

BERNIE. Yes, I can imagine. And who told you to ask for me?

MEGAN. My mother. Darlene Woods? Do you remember her?

BERNIE. I can't place the name.

MEGAN. Well, she hasn't been here in twenty-two years. But she stayed at this hotel when she was my age and she said you and your wife were very nice to her. Does *this* seem familiar to you?

BERNIE. No.

MEGAN. She wanted to be an actress? She didn't make it but she said you put her picture up on the wall. It didn't help her any and eventually she came home….

BERNIE. … So what would you like me to do?

MEGAN. I don't know. I'll be very honest with you. I thought I'd be excited getting here today, but I'm not. I'm overwhelmed…. I mean I don't know a single soul in New York except for your name…. Do you still have her picture up?

BERNIE. I don't know. Some I keep up. Some I change. Some are on the other wall…. Let's look…. *(She wipes her eyes with her hand.)* You need a handkerchief?

MEGAN. *(Tearfully.)* Oh, no thanks. I have a dozen of them in my lost suitcase.

BERNIE. Here we are.

(They stand in front of the wall of eight-by-ten headshots. She looks up and down … then:)

MEGAN. Oh, my God. That's her. That's my mother…. She's up on a wall in New York. I'm so impressed…. Do you remember her now?

BERNIE. I'm really trying.

MEGAN. She wanted to stick it out here but getting a job as an actress in New York was really hard back then.

BERNIE. And always will be.

MEGAN. Instead she went back to Ohio and had me.

BERNIE. So she had a hit in Ohio. What's wrong with that?

MEGAN. But if they can find my luggage and I can get my room, I'm here to stay.... As an actress, I mean.... Eventually.... And you won't have to put my picture up on this wall.... I'm sorry. That came out wrong.

BERNIE. It's alright. These were the Unknown Actors. Better your picture should be outside a theater.

MEGAN. I'm all prepared. I have the name of an acting coach and I've got a small job set up. It doesn't pay much but I don't need much.

BERNIE. Except lunch. My treat. Come on.... If you want to sit with your mother, I'll bring her picture over.

MEGAN. Oh, no. Leave it where it is. She's very proud to be up there.... Is it alright if I had a tuna salad? It was my mother's favorite.

BERNIE. Tuna just like your mother. Only fresher. I'll call the hotel about your room....

(BERNIE exits to kitchen.)

MEGAN. Thank you. Grow up, Megan, grow up.

(She sits looking lonely and takes out a small camera. She takes a picture of the restaurant. It flashes. MICKEY puts up his hand.)

MICKEY. Please don't. I get that everywhere.... *(To ANDREW.)* Were you listening? Every kid comes to New York to be discovered. Not me. You want to know who discovered me? The truth?

ANDREW. Who?

MICKEY. I did. I hoid myself working in a small club one night and I thought, "Hey! I'm terrific. I never hoid anyone so funny. I swear to God, just like that I appeared outa the blue.... And if I wasn't there that night, I never would have discovered me.

ANDREW. Did you worry about your accent?

MICKEY. What accent? It's not an accent. It's a local speech pattern.... *You* have an accent.... *(The rain has stopped. The sun comes out. BERNIE comes out of the kitchen with a plate of tuna salad and a drink. To BERNIE.)* Bernie, when you get a chance, try to notice how our tongues are hanging out.

BERNIE. I'll be right with you. *(He puts the salad and drink on MEGAN's table.)* Very fresh. My wife caught the tuna this morning.

MEGAN. Mom told me how generous you and your wife were to her.... She told me that when she left to go back to Ohio, she owed you eighteen dollars and thirty cents. *(Takes out a check.)* Here's a check from her. Now she's all paid up.

BERNIE. Suddenly the whole world is paying me back.... Keep it. You'll need it in New York.

MEGAN. Really? *(He nods.)* Well, I could use it till they find my suitcase.... But I'll pay you back then.

BERNIE. Please. I'm trying to get out of the banking business.

MEGAN. Thanks so much.... I was hoping I'd see some celebrities when I came in.

BERNIE. It's your lucky day.... You see the man on the left? One of the funniest people in the world. A huge star.... That's Mickey Fox.

MEGAN. He is?... I never heard of him.

BERNIE. Shh. Don't let him know. He's sensitive.

MEGAN. Wow. I'm here ten minutes and I'm sitting near one of the biggest stars in the world.... What was his name again?

BERNIE. Mickey Fox.

MEGAN. Right. Bernie? Could I take a picture of us? *(She takes out her camera.)* To send to my mother?

BERNIE. Why not?

MEGAN. She'll love this.

(She stands next to BERNIE, holds camera at arm's length, puts her head next to his and clicks the flash.)

MICKEY. That's the last one, alright?

(SOLOMAN comes in through the lobby door. He stands there.)

SOLOMAN. Excuse me. I'm sure I can think of some way to settle this.

BERNIE. *(Aside.)* Oy gut. He's back.

MEGAN. He looks like an actor. Is he?

BERNIE. No. He writes plays.

MEGAN. *(Impressed.)* He does? Is he good?

BERNIE. He owes me four dollars and eighty cents.... Excuse me. *(He crosses to SOLOMAN.)* You can sit, you can go, just keep out of my way. I've got customers here.

(BERNIE walks away. SOLOMAN sits down, not too far from MEGAN. She smiles, he acknowledges with a slight nod.)

MICKEY. Bernie!

(He chokes himself to show hunger.)

BERNIE. I'll be with you in a minute, Mickey. I promise.

(MEGAN is waiting for a chance to say something to SOLOMAN.... She plunges in.)

MEGAN. Hello.

SOLOMAN. *(Wary. He doesn't want trouble.)* Hello.

MEGAN. Er, would ... would you mind if I introduced myself?

SOLOMAN. *(Nervous.)* Please don't take me wrong, but for what purpose?

MEGAN. No purpose.... I've had a rough day, and I'm glad to be here in this coffee shop.... Bernie, the one you were just talking to? He's very nice.... It's an interesting place, isn't it?

SOLOMAN. To be honest, I have conflicting feelings.

MEGAN. Well, my name is Megan Woods.

SOLOMAN. Yes. *(He looks away, then feels obliged to answer.)* Soloman Mantutu.

MEGAN. Oh!! You're the playwright, aren't you?

SOLOMAN. *(In total amazement.) You've heard of me??*

MEGAN. Well, I'm an actress ... sort of.... I try to keep up with all the playwrights and what they're doing.

SOLOMAN. It's amazing that you tracked me down.

MEGAN. Actually, Bernie told me who you were.

SOLOMAN. He did?... How generous of him.

MEGAN. He's been *extremely* generous to me.... He bought me lunch.

SOLOMAN. Oh?... He gave me cake. Did he give you cake as well?

MEGAN. No. Well, I'm not a famous playwright.... By the way, Megan Woods is my real name. Some people think I made it up to make it sound more theatrical.

SOLOMAN. I see. My real name is Soloman Mantutu.

MEGAN. It's a beautiful and unusual name.

SOLOMAN. You think so? In South Africa there are thousands of Solomans. Soloman in Africa is like Jimmy in New York ... Or Baby in California.

BERNIE. *(Out of kitchen, crosses to MICKEY.)* I'm so sorry, Mickey.

MICKEY. Foist, say hello to Andrew Duncan, maybe the most important producer in London, as you call tell from his tweed suit.... Andrew, dis is Bernie, owner of the finest restaurant in the city. One day I'll take you there.

(ANDREW laughs.)

BERNIE. Very nice to meet you.

MICKEY. Wait'll he finishes laughing....

ANDREW. *(Still laughing.)* Pleasure to meet you, Bernie.

MICKEY. Are you two gonna talk all day? I'm hungry. *(Looking at menu ...)* We'll have a number two ... we'll share a number six ... we'll split a number ten ... give him a side order of number eight ... and I'll have a taste of number twelve.... And give us each a peach cobbler.... Cut it in half. He'll have the peach, I'll have the cobbler.... Tell the cobbler not to make the shoes too tight.

(ANDREW laughs heartily, BERNIE doesn't.)

ANDREW. *(To BERNIE.)* Don't you find everything he says funny?

BERNIE. Yes. But we don't have any peach cobbler today.... Excuse me. *(BERNIE crosses to SOLOMAN. To SOLOMAN, out of MEGAN's earshot.)* How much would it cost to end this relationship?

SOLOMAN. *(Takes worn manuscript from his tattered leather bag.)* Please read my play.... I'm not asking for your opinion or your help.... I just want the satisfaction that one compassionate person in this country has read my work.... Then I can go home and tell my wife and family that my play has received an audience ... that someone has heard my voice ... because the joy is not in the result ... but in the doing. *(He holds out script.)* Please take it and I'll go.

BERNIE. Mr. Mantutu.... I don't even see plays. I don't like musicals.... I like to read books. Books are quiet ... and when you finish them, they don't ask if you liked them.... But, I'll give you some advice.... Get into politics. You'll be President of South Africa one day.... Goodbye, Mr. Soloman.

(BERNIE walks away. SOLOMAN watches him, then leaves the script on an empty table near the register. He flattens and smoothes it down first.... He's about to leave when he sees MEGAN and crosses back to her.)

SOLOMAN. *(To MEGAN.)* It was very nice meeting you Meganwoods.

MEGAN. It's two names. Megan and Woods.

SOLOMAN. Oh. I wish you well as an actress.

(SOLOMAN starts to go.)

MEGAN. Wait!... Could you tell me which plays you wrote?

SOLOMAN. I actually only finished one. I was brought to New York to have it produced. "The Shadows of Africa."

MEGAN. Great title.... Where can I get a copy of it?

SOLOMAN. *(Points.)* Over there on that counter.... I've left it for Mr. Bernie to read. There are no published copies yet.

MEGAN. Well, when it's published, I'd love to see it.

SOLOMAN. I would too.... Goodbye Megan ... and Woods.

MEGAN. *(Gets up holding camera.)* Could I just take a picture of you?

SOLOMAN. I'm not looking very happy now.

MEGAN. You will. One day.

(MEGAN quickly takes the picture, flash.)

MICKEY. Enough is enough.

SOLOMAN. Goodbye.

(SOLOMAN leaves. MEGAN goes back to her salad. From the lobby door, two women enter. They are ARLEEN and CINDY. BERNIE enters from the kitchen.)

ARLEEN. ... When I was a little girl and went to the theater, people always dressed nicely.... Did you see that couple behind us yesterday? The husband was wearing swimming trunks, I swear to God.

CINDY. What about the wife? She came in on rollerblades.... They made her take them off but she was spinning the wheels during the show.

ARLEEN. And then I got absolutely nauseous when they took out the corn on the cob.... Buttering it with their fingers.... Six people moved up to the balcony.... Don't they have a sign about that?

CINDY. No. You're just not allowed to take your drinks back to your seat. No one ever figured they'd bring in corn on the cob.

ARLEEN. I'd put a sign up about everything. No corn on the cob, no fried calamari, and no won-ton soup.

CINDY. Oh, and what about their little boy? Kicking my seat during the entire show ... until his legs went through the back of his seat. He couldn't get out and they didn't say a word.

ARLEEN. That wasn't their little boy. *His* mother just put him in there and left to go shopping.

BERNIE. *(To ARLEEN and CINDY.)* Just the two of you?

ARLEEN. No, three. Oh my God I left my mother in the parking lot.

(ARLEEN exits. CINDY shrugs and follows ARLEEN off.
From the street door, two people enter. They are elderly. The woman is RAYLEEN, of indeterminate age. Her face has so much makeup on, it's hard to know what she really looks like. She wears a very bad wig, mostly blondish, more orangey. It sits high and comes down below her neck. She wears a fur coat, knee length. And boots. The fur, if that's what it is, seems to be made of pieces of fur from every animal ever found, Strips of mink, squirrel, white cat, gray dog and maybe a pinto horse. Yet she wears it well, with style. Her companion, CHARLES, just stands there waiting for someone to attend them. ANDREW, who is facing her, sees her first.)

ANDREW. Good God, who is that?

MICKEY. *(Turns and looks.)* I don't know. Could be Harpo Marx's mother, who knows?... Maybe a retired actress.... She put all her costumes together and made that coat.... Poisonally I feel badly.

ANDREW. For her?

MICKEY. For him. This could be a blind date.

RAYLEEN. *(Smoothes CHARLES' lapel with her hand.)* Oh, Charles, not this tie. *(She straightens it.)* Never wear dark green for lunch.

ANDREW. I've never in my life seen fur like that.

MICKEY. Maybe it's not fur. It could be the toupees of all her former lovers. *(He turns away.)* Listen, better not stare at her.

ANDREW. Sorry. Very impolite of me.

MICKEY. It's not that. But who knows what it could do to your eyes. *(They turn away. BERNIE comes in from the kitchen, sees the couple.)* Bernie.... Hey, who is that? With one coat, she cleaned out the Bronx Zoo.

BERNIE. *(Aside to MICKEY.)* Comes in here two, maybe three times a year. Same coat, same man. Acts like it's a fancy French restaurant. Always tells me she made a reservation. A reservation in a coffee shop.... Excuse me. *(He crosses to them. To RAYLEEN.)* Hello. How are you?

RAYLEEN. *(A very cultured voice. An attitude of coming from money or society.)* Very well, thank you. We called for a reservation last night. A corner table for two. Not too close to the sun's glare. I believe Charles spoke to you.

BERNIE. I have your table waiting.

(BERNIE walks, they don't follow.)

RAYLEEN. No tablecloth? We never dine without a tablecloth.... Can you imagine, Charles?

BERNIE. I'll take care of it. Please sit. It'll just take a second.

RAYLEEN. I'm not in the habit of sitting more than once during dinner.

BERNIE. I'll be as quick as I can. *(He rushes off into kitchen.)* Oy-oy-oy.

RAYLEEN. Your eyes are wandering.... Look at me, Charles, it's Rayleen.... Are you alright?... Smile for me.... Come on, smile. *(He looks blankly at her.)* That's better. *(She turns, sees MEGAN at a table.)* Miss? What kind of cigarettes do you carry here?

MEGAN. I—I don't know.

RAYLEEN. I don't think that's the right answer, darling. Keep on your toes. *(Aside to CHARLES.)* Charles, I'm going to trim your mustache today. It's getting very walrussy. And don't argue about it.... *(She snaps her fingers in his face.)* Wandering.... You're wandering again, dear.

MICKEY. *(To ANDREW.)* I'll tell you what I think.... I think they were on their way to a big party in South Hampton and their Zeppelin had a flat tire.

(ANDREW laughs, covering his mouth.
BERNIE comes in with a plain tablecloth, puts it on table. Beckons to RAYLEEN that it's ready. CHARLES starts but she stops him.)

RAYLEEN. Stay Charles. We'll wait till we're shown our table.

(BERNIE hears it, rushes to them.)

BERNIE. I'm ready for you now.

RAYLEEN. Oh, you didn't have to put yourself out for us. *(She takes CHARLES' hand and leads him. She passes MICKEY's table and stops. To MICKEY.)* Is that you, Robert?... Charles, it's Robert.... We were just talking about you....

MICKEY. She thinks I'm Robert.

ANDREW. Who's Robert?

MICKEY. Shh. Don't get her upset. You'll end up in the coat.

RAYLEEN. And how is Genevieve?

MICKEY. Genevieve? Genevieve is fine, thank you.

RAYLEEN. Please give her our love. Darling woman. *(She laughs. To CHARLES.)* What did she ever see in him?

(CHARLES never says anything. BERNIE pulls out the chair for her.)

BERNIE. I'll get your menus.

RAYLEEN. No, no. I know it by heart ... but refresh me. *(She laughs, looks at CHARLES.)* I said it again, didn't I, Charles? *(To BERNIE.)* Charles always loves it when I say refresh me ... so refresh me.

MICKEY. *(Aside to ANDREW.)* My last guess? "Sunset Boulevard." He's the dead monkey.

BERNIE. The menu changed again today. I'll get it.

(He goes, passing MICKEY.)

RAYLEEN. *(She hums "I Love Paris.")* Da da da da da da da dum. Da da da da dadum.... Sing it with me, Charles.

BERNIE. You hear?

(CHARLES picks up silver, looks at it.)

RAYLEEN. Don't play with the silverware, Charles. You never know where it's been.

MICKEY. *(To ANDREW.)* Enough of that. Tell me again.

ANDREW. Well, it's plain and simple.... We want you to come to London and star in a revival of "Fiddler on the Roof." ... You as Tevya.

MICKEY. I can't believe my ears. Tevya! My God, what a part. You don't know how flattered I am. How honored I am. Maybe the greatest show ever written. All my life I've been waiting for someone to ask me to do something like this.

ANDREW. *(Beaming.)* I'm *so* glad you feel that way.

MICKEY. I'll tell you why it's a lousy idea. What the hell do I need it for?

ANDREW. But you'd be wonderful.

MICKEY. That I know. But I woik alone. What do I need forty dancers getting in my way? The audience would stand up saying, "Where is he? I can't see him." Oh, I admit the songs are beautiful. "Sunrise, sunset, we grow old, we die, I've grown accustomed to our shtetl." ... My audience doesn't want to see me in a classic.

ANDREW. I see what you mean.

MICKEY. Don't give up. I can be persuaded.

(BERNIE comes back and gives RAYLEEN their menus and some flowers in a small vase.)

BERNIE. I found some flowers in the back. It's not much, I know.

RAYLEEN. Oh, Charles, you didn't forget.... I knew you wouldn't.... And do you remember what you said to me as we came out of the show that night?... Do you? Do you, dear?... *THINK!! (She shivers. To BERNIE.)* Is that a draft I feel in here?

BERNIE. It's the air conditioner. It's almost ninety-five today.

RAYLEEN. I wouldn't know. I'm always cold. *(Pulls coat around her.)* Could you please shut it off at this end of the room?

BERNIE. It doesn't work that way. It's all one room. *(SOLOMAN comes in through the lobby door. To RAYLEEN.)* I'll see what I can do. Excuse me. *(Passing MICKEY.)* Why in my place? Why? Why? *(Seeing SOLOMON.)* WHAT??? What now??

SOLOMAN. I'm here to settle my bill. *(He takes a bill out of his pocket.)* Here is five dollars. Thank you for your patience.

BERNIE. You didn't have it ten minutes ago. Now you have five dollars.

SOLOMAN. I did have it ten minutes ago. I was saving to put towards my fare back home. But since five dollars is a long way from the money I need, I decided to clear my debts first.

BERNIE. Why would I be interested in this information? You're planting seeds aren't you, Mr. Soloman? Well, I'm sorry, but nothing grows on 46th Street. Keep your five dollars and goodbye.

(BERNIE stuffs it in SOLOMAN's pocket and turns to go.)

SOLOMAN. If you don't want my money, I'm not going to make it my life's work. *(He holds out the bill.)* Yes or no?

(RAYLEEN taps on her glass with a spoon to get BERNIE's attention. He looks at her, then looks back at SOLOMAN.)

BERNIE. I've got a customer waiting. Stay here and then we'll finish this off forever. *(He goes back to RAYLEEN's table as SOLOMAN sits. To RAYLEEN.)* I'm very sorry. It's a busy day.

RAYLEEN. I understand but Charles is wasting into thin air.... A pot of tea to start, please.

BERNIE. Yes. A pot of tea. And to eat?

RAYLEEN. Let me tell you how to make it. I want it made with two bags.

BERNIE. Two bags. Right.

RAYLEEN. The first bag, orange pekoe dark, should be placed in the pot first. The pot should be pre-warmed for three minutes.

BERNIE. Certainly.... Now we have two specials today.

RAYLEEN. Then I want the tea steeped for two and a half minutes. The second tea bag, either a light chamomile or a jasmine, is placed *in* the pot for a minute and a half. No longer because I don't want the chamomile or the jasmine to overpower the orange pekoe. You understand?

BERNIE. Completely.

RAYLEEN. Also I would like the cup and saucer preheated as well. That's the trick, you see.

BERNIE. That I never thought of.

RAYLEEN. You do have China, I assume.

BERNIE. Chinese tea?

RAYLEEN. Your dishes. Are your dishes China?

BERNIE. I could look and see. It's a nice white cup and saucer. Never breaks.

RAYLEEN. White doesn't absorb heat very well.... Do you have honey?

BERNIE. Honey? Yes. We have honey.

RAYLEEN. I don't like honey. The texture is too thick.... Be sure to warm the cup and saucer at room temperature.

BERNIE. I'll check it with the thermostat.... Is that all you want?

RAYLEEN. Yes.... I don't like the tablecloth. Don't you have linen?

BERNIE. It's a tablecloth. To tell the truth, it's not a tablecloth restaurant.... I don't mean to be rude, but—

RAYLEEN. How do you prepare your chicken?

BERNIE. We cook it.... I've got a very good cook in there—

RAYLEEN. Charles doesn't eat starch or fats.

BERNIE. All our tea is nonfat. *(He rubs his arms.)* You're right. It is cold in here. Let me fix the air conditioner. I'll be right back. What does she want from me?

(He walks directly to SOLOMAN. MICKEY and ANDREW watch BERNIE pass them.)

RAYLEEN. *(To CHARLES.)* Now Charles, where were we? Oh yes ... J.B. ... An actor. He was in "Don Juan." ... Go.

(RAYLEEN puts a timer down.)

BERNIE. *(Rushes to SOLOMAN.)* Do you want a job? Part time?

SOLOMAN. I'm not asking you for that.

BERNIE. And I didn't ask you to write a play that didn't get produced. You want to job?

SOLOMAN. I could use work, yes.

BERNIE. I need a waiter. Maybe a hour, a day, a week. I don't know how long these people are going to stay.

SOLOMAN. And the salary?

BERNIE. We'll discuss it later.

(BERNIE is about to turn.)

SOLOMAN. I don't want to trade off my financial obligations for a job that underpays me.

BERNIE. Underpays you? You're not even a union member.

SOLOMAN. I don't want to break any union laws.

BERNIE. I'll explain it to them. They owe me a favor. Everybody in this neighborhood owes me a favor. *What more do you want me to do?* Alright, I'll read your goddamn play.

SOLOMAN. In your present mood, I don't think you'd be receptive to my play.

BERNIE. I'll make myself receptive ... give me the play. *(To RAYLEEN.)* My waiter just got here. He'll be with you in a minute. *(To SOLOMAN.)* Come on.

(BERNIE and SOLOMAN go into kitchen.)

MICKEY. *(To ANDREW.)* ... Besides, if I did Tevya, everybody would think I'm pushing da Jewish thing too much.... Although only fifty per cent of my audience is Jewish.... The other half sits *next* to the Jews so someone can tell them what the show's about.

(ANDREW laughs.)

RAYLEEN. *(To CHARLES.)* Charles? Remember when they had dancing in here?... Eddie Duchin and his orchestra, wasn't it?... And it was three times this size. And it was on the East Side.... Things change so quickly these days.... And our conversations have lost something, I think....

(SOLOMAN comes out with a white waiter's jacket with a small pin-on bow tie. He crosses to RAYLEEN's table.)

SOLOMAN. My name is Soloman. I am your waiter.

RAYLEEN. Yes, Soloman.... I'm so glad you're still here.

MICKEY. *(Aside to ANDREW.)* Aha! It's Sheena the Jungle Woman, eighty years later.

(ANDREW tries to laugh quietly and slaps MICKEY's arm to stop.)

SOLOMAN. May I have your order, please?

RAYLEEN. *(As if she never said it.)* I want a pot of tea. And I want it with two bags.

SOLOMAN. *(Writing on a pad.)* Two bags are always the best way, m'am.

RAYLEEN. The first bag, orange pekoe, should be placed in the pot first.

SOLOMAN. So it becomes the dominant flavor, I understand.

RAYLEEN. *(Smiles warmly at him.)* Yes.... Very good.... I've always remembered that smile of yours.... *(We hear the telephone ring in the kitchen.)* Now then, the pot should be pre-warmed for three minutes.

SOLOMAN. The tea leaves usually react very well to that.

(The phone rings again.)

RAYLEEN. And I would like half a lemon on its own dish.... Slightly squeezed with the top lemon pits tossed aside.

SOLOMAN. But of course, madam.

(BERNIE comes out halfway.)

BERNIE. *(Calls out.)* Young lady? Megan? *(MEGAN turns.)*

Your mother's on the phone from Ohio. Take it here.

(BERNIE goes back in. MEGAN rushes to the register.)

RAYLEEN. *(She heard that. To SOLOMAN.)* They treat the help too well these days, don't you think Soloman?

SOLOMAN. Times change, madam.

RAYLEEN. Exactly.

MEGAN. *(On the phone, excited.)*.You knew I'd be here, didn't you?... Yes, your picture's still on the wall. You look just the same. *(Lowers her voice.)* This place is so cool, Mom.... On my first day I meet Mickey Fox, the comedian, and Soloman Mantutu, the playwright.... Mantutu.... Well, you will one day.

(MEGAN turns her back so she can talk more privately.)

MICKEY. *(To ANDREW.)* ... On the other hand, I might do "My Fair Lady." ... Listen to this ... I'm Professor Higgins ... only instead of teaching Eliza how to speak English, I'll teach her to speak like *I* speak.... Dot's funny.... Dat my audience would like.... "Da Rain in Spain is woise than a sunboin in Toikey." Dat's a hit.

(BLACKOUT.)

Scene 2
"Autumn"

(A few months later. About 5 P.M. Just turning dark.
Two women sit at a table drinking coffee. They are ARLEEN and CINDY.)

ARLEEN. Just tell me why that show today got good reviews. What was good about it? I thought it sucked.

CINDY. I never heard you use that word before.

ARLEEN. I have a fourteen-year-old daughter. Either you join them or you lose them.

CINDY. You saw nothing redeeming about this play?

ARLEEN. No and I'll tell you why. It wasn't a play. It was two people talking. He said something, she said something, they said something and at the end, nobody said anything.

CINDY. And yet you laughed.

ARLEEN. I didn't say it wasn't funny. It was extremely funny. But it was stupid.... I enjoyed it, but I didn't like it.

CINDY. You laugh at stupid things?

ARLEEN. I have no taste. I can't help it.

CINDY. See, I didn't like the play but for another reason.... It was fraudulent. It was an unfulfilled abstraction.... I found it hypothetical, theoretical, disengaging and unbearably abstruse.

ARLEEN. I read the same review. I never agree with him.

(They both sip their coffee at the same time as SOLOMAN comes out carrying two plates of cake.)

SOLOMAN. Ladies ....

(He puts down the plates.)

ARLEEN. What's this?

SOLOMAN. Pound cake, m'am. Freshly baked.

CINDY. We didn't order this.

SOLOMAN. With our compliments. Only on Wednesdays.

ARLEEN. I feel guilty. We only ordered coffee.

SOLOMAN. I have no wish to make you feel guilty.

(SOLOMAN starts to reach for the plate.)

ARLEEN. *(She pulls it back.)* I'll live with it.

CINDY. From what I heard, this is more than just a coffee shop.

SOLOMAN. Oh, yes. We serve dishes you will not find in most coffee shops. Things I've never eaten before for which I've acquired a great taste.

ARLEEN. For example?

SOLOMAN. A special dish called cheese blintzes. Have you heard of it?

CINDY. We grew up on it. What's so special?

SOLOMAN. Well, for a South African like me, it was a great treat. Although back home we are starting to get bagels.... I like them but you have to get used to the chewing.

CINDY. You have a wonderful way of expressing yourself. You sound like an actor. Are you?

SOLOMAN. *(Smiles.)* Oh, no. No, I could never be an actor. I don't have the talent for that.... No, actually I'm a playwright. *(The GIRLS look at each other.)* And a teacher ... and now a waiter.

ARLEEN. How do you find time to do all that?

SOLOMAN. By not doing the playwrighting or the teaching.... But my day will come.

CINDY. I'm sure it will.

SOLOMAN. By the way ... have you heard of kreplak?

ARLEEN. Krepla*ch*.... It's a ch sound at the end. Like clearing your throat.

SOLOMAN. Kreplachchchchch.

CINDY. Now you got it.

SOLOMAN. I like kreplachchchchch very much.... They're like fortune cookies without the fortune. *(They laugh.... He leaves.)* Kreplachchchchch.

(He's gone.)

CINDY. Sweet.

ARLEEN. I enjoyed him more than the play.

(MICKEY FOX enters from the street door. He takes off his raincoat and hangs it up. The two women spot him.)

ARLEEN. Oh, my God. Cindy, look. It's Mickey Fox.

CINDY. *(Turns.)* Is that him?

MICKEY. *(To women as he hangs up his coat.)* It's true. It's him.

He's hanging up his coat.... Hello. How are you? Nice to see you.

ARLEEN. We just want to tell you we love you to death.

MICKEY. Well, I appreciate that opportunity. Thank you.

(MICKEY sits.)

CINDY. My husband knows every one of your routines by heart.

MICKEY. Good. Tell him to send me a check. I don't want to bring a lawyer into this.

ARLEEN. Did you just think of that?

MICKEY. No. I had a hunch you were coming.

CINDY. We didn't see the show you're doing now but we intend to come.

MICKEY. Oh, well, this month we're sold out. Completely. You could go all over town, you won't find a ticket to this show.

CINDY. So we can't get in?

MICKEY. Unless you go to the box office. He's got racks of seats....

(MICKEY smiles, turns away.)

ARLEEN. *(Aside to CINDY.)* I thought he only talked like that on the stage.

(ZELDA, Bernie's wife, easily seventy-two but still strong and vital, enters . She really runs the place. She usually keeps one hand on her hip as she talks, a very feisty woman. She puts a plate of soup on MICKEY's table.)

ZELDA. *(The same accent as BERNIE.)* I want you to eat this soup, you hear? No back talk Mr. Big Shot. You look tired. Have you been sleeping?

MICKEY. Yes, but I can't mention any names....

ZELDA. *(Hits him with her napkin.)* Don't be a wise guy with me.... So are you going to London?

MICKEY. Not yet. I'm not doing "Fiddler" but I may do

"Phantom of the Opera" if they can woik out the problem.

ZELDA. What problem?

MICKEY. They need a mask to cover my mouth so no one can hear how I talk.... Zelda, sit down a minute. I've got great news for you.

ZELDA. If I sit down, I feel like I'm taking the day off. *(She sits.)* So what's the good news?

MICKEY. I met a woman. I think I'm in love. She's coming to see the show *again* tonight.

ZELDA. You're serious?

MICKEY. This one is something special. I immediately felt a something between us.

ZELDA. What kind of something?

MICKEY. I can't find the woids. A pie in the sky hit my eye something. My feet skipped a beat in the street something.... When did I ever say anything so stupid?...

ZELDA. You should do it more.

MICKEY. I'm seeing her tonight after the show. In twenty-five years I've never been this noivous.

ZELDA. How old is she?

MICKEY. She's a woman. A grown woman. A mature woman.... Twenty-six, twenty-seven, who knows?

ZELDA. So what do you like about her?

MICKEY. That she's not sixty-eight, sixty-nine.

(ZELDA gets up.)

ZELDA. You never know how to pick the right woman.

MICKEY. What about my ex-wife?... She was the right woman. The right woman for the right lawyer. He made a fortune from me.

SOLOMAN. *(Comes out of kitchen.)* Mr. Fox. Telephone. You want it in here or back there? It's a Miss Belinda.

MICKEY. Back there.

SOLOMAN. When can we talk about you know what?

MICKEY As soon as I take this call ... I think I'm in love, Soloman.

SOLOMAN. That's good. A man shouldn't go through life without a woman.

MICKEY. I don't. But being in love is good too.

(SOLOMAN and MICKEY go. ZELDA crosses to the cash register, checks out receipts.)

ARLEEN. *(To CINDY.)* You know what I never saw?

CINDY. What?

ARLEEN. "Cats." It was there how long? Fifteen years? And I never saw it.

CINDY. How come?

ARLEEN. If I don't see something in the first five years, I lose interest.

CINDY. I know what you mean .... *(MEGAN comes in through lobby door.)* No matter how good the reviews, I miss so many Shakespeare plays.

ARLEEN. That's different. He's been around over four hundred years. He's not going anywhere....

CINDY. I don't like to see Shakespeare in a theater. I like to see Shakespeare in the park.

ARLEEN. What's the difference?

CINDY. If it rains, I get home early.

(There are a few people sitting at the counter. [Use people whenever you can.] MEGAN carries her shoulder bag filled with paperback plays. She is not the happy girl we met in the first scene. She walks past ZELDA and sits in her usual spot.)

ZELDA. *(Without looking up from receipts.)* So, Megan, what's wrong with you today?

MEGAN. ... Why do you think something is wrong?

ZELDA. Every day you walk in here it's birds are singing. Today nothing.... So I figure something is wrong.

MEGAN. Not something. *Everything.* I am in so far over my head.

ZELDA. So you had a bad day in acting class. That's why you go there, right?

MEGAN. I'm not sure *why* I go there.... Being an actress is my mother's dream, not mine.

ZELDA. No? Then what's your dream.

MEGAN. ... I have a boyfriend back home. He's going to med school.... We were going to get engaged but my mother thought I was rushing it.... She said, "Go to New York first. Experience your own life before jumping into marriage."

ZELDA. It's not a bad idea. Bernie waited for me.

MEGAN. He did? .... How long?

ZELDA. Five, ten minutes. I was taking a shower.... Stick with the acting for a while.... If I wanted to be an actress, Bernie would have waited.

MEGAN. I guess you're right.... I'm not a quitter, Zelda. Honestly.

ZELDA. I know.

MEGAN. I know you know. You're not a quitter either.... My mother told me about your childhood. You and Bernie. What you went through.... I'm sorry. I shouldn't have said that.

ZELDA. It's alright. I'll tell you.... Yes, we were in Poland when we were kids. In the camps. And we got out.... And here we are now, you and me talking.... So in a sense, I had a bad day too ... and this place was my dream.... Okay?

MEGAN. Okay.

(ZELDA leaves. MEGAN watcher her, then takes out her paperback plays. MICKEY comes out of the kitchen, crosses and sits at his table.)

MICKEY. What was I thinking?

ZELDA. *(To MICKEY.)* She's not coming?

MICKEY. No, she's coming. She asked for an extra seat for her fiancé.

ZELDA. Never mind. One day you're going to find the right woman.

MICKEY. Next time I'll look for someone my own age ... 30,

31, like that. Where's Bernie?

ZELDA. He's visiting his mother.

MICKEY. His mother is still alive? How is that possible?

ZELDA. She gave up smoking.

(ZELDA goes back into the kitchen. SOLOMAN sticks his head out.)

SOLOMAN. I'll be right with you, Mr. Fox.

(SOLOMAN goes back in.)

ARLEEN. In musicals, why must they wear those telephone operator things on their heads?

CINDY. It's from those rock concerts. Kids like their music loud.

ARLEEN. But then they can't hear the words.

CINDY. They don't come for the words. Words went out years ago.

ARLEEN. I have a rule. If there's a lot of dancing in a musical, I don't sit in the front row.

CINDY. Why's that?

ARLEEN. They sweat on you....

CINDY. In the ballet too?

ARLEEN. No, the ballerinas don't sweat.... Only the guys that pick them up.

CINDY. Same thing at the opera. Pavarotti spits on the first three rows....

CINDY and ARLEEN. Ewww ....

(MEGAN pours over a play, then looks up at MICKEY.)

MEGAN. Mr. Fox? I know I have a lot of nerve asking this, but are you busy?

MICKEY. Busy? No. I'm booked but I'm not busy.... Why?

MEGAN. Do you know much about Shakespeare?

MICKEY. A little.... He was a playwright, I think.... Mostly Off Broadway.... He lived at the Stratford Hotel.... Some people think he didn't write all those plays.... If this is true, how come he could afford a nice two-story house with the river in the back? This is a fact because you know how much a thatched roof cost in those days? Ask Margaret Thatcher, that's how she made her money.... The mix-up was because they spelled Shakespeare's name so many ways then.... Shakespeare, Shakes*pore*, *Shook*spare, Shockspoin, Shickstein.... In those days everyone was a Shakespeare.

MEGAN. Can I use that in my class?

MICKEY. Too late. I just decided to use it in my act.

MEGAN. The trouble is, I love everything he writes, but I don't understand it all.

MICKEY. Nobody in the woild ever did.... "The shard-bone beetle with his drowsy hums hath rung nights yawning peal." Do you think two people met on the street and one said, "Hey, how are you?" and the other one said, "Ah, the shard-bone beetle with his drowsy hums, hath rung nights yawning peal." ... And the foist one says, "I'm sorry to hear it." ... And the critics don't have the noive to contradict it.... Shakespeare put down whatever he wanted and said, "Let the audience figure it out. I'm busy."

MEGAN. But maybe that's the way people spoke in those days.

MICKEY. Only if you wanted to get a part in his play....

(MEGAN puts her books in bag, gets up.)

MEGAN. Well, I going to my singing class. Any tips?

MICKEY. Stay away from "Ol' Man River."

MEGAN. I will.

MICKEY. Hey! Remember, I left you two seats for tonight's show.

MEGAN. Make it one. I couldn't find anyone to go with.

MICKEY. I'll go with you. I haven't watched myself on stage in a long time.

MEGAN. God, I wish I had your confidence.

(MEGAN goes.)

ARLEEN. *(To CINDY.)* Let me ask you a question.

CINDY. What?

ARLEEN. Do you understand Irish plays?... I sat in the first row, I couldn't understand a word they said.

CINDY. You have to try and listen slower.

ARLEEN. ... I do. But every time I get a word or two, they're five sentences ahead of me.

CINDY. The original Irish cast leaves after six months. Wait until the Americans replace them.

(SOLOMAN comes out of the kitchen carrying a plate. He puts it down in front of MICKEY.)

SOLOMAN. Whitefish on a sesame bagel. Compliments of Soloman.

MICKEY. Uh huh. I feel a bribe coming on.

SOLOMAN. On no. Mr. Fox. All I want from you is honesty.... Did you finish the play?

MICKEY. Sit down.... It's alright. *(SOLOMAN sits anxiously.)* Yes. I finished it. *(He reaches back into his coat and takes out SOLOMAN's play.)* Last night.... Two in the morning.... Soloman Soloman Soloman, what a piece of woik.

SOLOMAN. I can admit to you that my hand is shaking.... Then you liked it?

MICKEY. Liked it? I said Soloman three times, didn't I? This is a serious piece. Dis came from a deep place inside you.

SOLOMAN. Every word.

MICKEY. Every word, every sentence, every page, there's your blood pouring all over it.

SOLOMAN. Yes. And that comes through?

MICKEY. More or less.

SOLOMAN. Oh. You just took two Solomans away.... Do you think you understand the play? Do you appreciate what this man had to deal with?

MICKEY. Do I know what it's like to be born in South Africa thirty-five years ago? No. But I see what advances are being made today. The blacks are running the government and the whites are becoming rap singers.

SOLOMAN. Mr. Fox, I know something is missing from my play. But I know South Africa. I know my people. What I *don't* know is how to reach a wider audience. When you talk so humorously on the stage about people of religious and racial backgrounds, you pull down the ethnic barriers for everyone. That is what I need in my play. To make it universal.

MICKEY. Now you're talking.

SOLOMAN. I never had the time to develop a sense of humor. But you make me laugh.... Sometimes in the kitchen I'm still laughing at what you said.

MICKEY. And you touch me, Soloman. You know why I get big laughs from an audience? Because I make them feel guilty. What you do is something different. You make them feel angry ... and that takes courage to do.

SOLOMAN. That's what I hoped for. Because if you relax an audience into passivity, it's much harder to arouse their conscience.

MICKEY. Well, I wouldn't arouse their conscience *too* much. There's people in the audience anxious to go home and have sex.

SOLOMAN. Oh, I am a great believer in sex.

MICKEY. Good. For this they'll pay money.

SOLOMAN. My play talks about the politics of sex, the religious distortion of sex and the use of power through sex.

MICKEY. I'm not so sure about the first two. But the *power* of sex appeals to a certain type of audience. They usually come Saturday night.

SOLOMAN. You amuse me the way you phrase things. I learn a great deal from your pragmatism.

MICKEY. I don't think I'm pragmatic. What I do is try to hit them in the kishkas.

SOLOMAN. Kishkas?... Is that like blintzes?

MICKEY. No. Kishkas is the stomach. The *pit* of the stomach. That's what you aim for.... When a man is sick, he holds his kishkas. When he laughs hard, he holds his kishkas.... The kishkas hold the key to your central noivous system.... Doctors don't know that. They give you pills, they give you an MRI, they test your PSA, they give you a cup, you fill it up, they put a stick here, a tube there.... But they overlook one thing. The kishkas. I know. I'm the foremost kishka man in the country.

SOLOMAN. So let me see if I understand what you're saying.

MICKEY. I wouldn't remember. Sometimes I get carried away.

SOLOMAN. I am too serious. Is that what you're saying? That I get into polemics too much?

MICKEY. That's possible. Because sometimes when your kishkas gets tied up into a knot so tight you can't stand it, you take a polemic.

SOLOMAN. I don't follow you.

MICKEY. You're better off.

SOLOMAN. No. This is so instructive. I'm trying to reach an audience in the very depth of their soul. And the kishkas is the metaphor for that soul. Is that what you mean?

MICKEY. Well, I don't think there's a metaphor for kishkas.... If you ever saw what it looked like, you wouldn't bring the subject up.... But if you got hit there, you'd know. It's that simple.

SOLOMAN. In other words, the simpler the language, the more they will listen. The less complicated the message, the clearer the thought.

MICKEY. Now you got it. Too many big woids, they fall asleep. If it rhymes, they wake up.... Take Shakespeare.... He understood.... The STRUMPET plays a TRUMPET ... HORATIO had FELLATIO.... They hear that, they'll buy season tickets.

SOLOMAN. Are you saying then, that I should write more poetically?

MICKEY. Not exactly. Because poetry not only gets them out of the theater, they also leave New York.

SOLOMAN. *(Writes on a napkin.)* I'm taking notes on all this.

MICKEY. *(Takes the script out of his coat pocket.)* Good. Don't forget to put down HORATIO had FELLATIO.

SOLOMAN. Well, I would never use that.

MICKEY. Who can tell? When you get out of town and you're in trouble, who knows.... Alright, let's go to the script. *(He opens it, turns pages.)* I'm starting on page twenty-eight.

SOLOMAN. Why on twenty-eight?

MICKEY. Because from one to twenty-seven, there's not a kishka in the play.

SOLOMAN. I'm sorry but the first twenty-eight pages took me a year to write. If we don't understand what happened to this man as a child, then we never understand his bitterness.

MICKEY. Put it someplace in the middle. Because the foist ten minutes people are coming in late. They're yelling in the dark, "What row are you in? I think you got my seats," "You're standing on my hat." ... You know what I do for the foist ten minutes? I don't come on. I come on in the *second* ten minutes.... Okay, next page.... Are these sentences all typing mistakes?

SOLOMAN. No. His speech is in Zulu.

MICKEY. Here we got a problem.... Tell me, Soloman, you think a lot of Zululians go to plays in New York?

SOLOMAN. Of course not. It's just three lines. And when he finishes it in Zulu, he repeats it in English.

MICKEY. Well, New York is a tough town. When they hear a man talking Zulu in a theatre, they go out and look for the pretzel man.... Tell me if I'm insulting you.

SOLOMAN. When I said I was looking for humor, I didn't specifically mean *your* humor.

MICKEY. I understand. If it's important, keep it. But on opening night keep a Zulu or two in the audience.

SOLOMAN. I want to be open, not stubborn. That's a fault of mine. Have you noticed?

MICKEY. Only when you talk.

ARLEEN. *(To CINDY.)* Have you ever noticed in the ads in the paper that there isn't a single show on Broadway that doesn't say, "The funniest show in town"?

CINDY. Well, they're not going to print the bad reviews, are they?

ARLEEN. I saw six ads that said "The funniest show in town." ... Only one can be the funniest.

CINDY. Would you go if it said, "The third funniest show in town"?

ARLEEN. Well, at least they're honest....

CINDY. I go to the first preview of a show because then I can make up my own mind.

ARLEEN. I do the same thing. I go to the first preview and think this is absolutely wonderful. And in the intermission I hear people say "This is a piece of crap" and I believe them.

MICKEY. *(To SOLOMAN.)* Look, I'm not a writer. I'm not a critic. But I'll say this. What you put down on paper, what you say about mankind, will be taught in schools one day.

SOLOMAN. Thank you but your praise is far, far too generous.

MICKEY. Of course, but what are friends for?

SOLOMAN. I'm glad you think of me as your friend.

MICKEY. A play about mankind is a touchy thing. People see it in the paper, they say, "Helen, don't get dressed. It's about mankind."

SOLOMAN. Yes, but don't you think that's a sad situation?

MICKEY. I find it unconscionable. But tell me what show you think they'll but tickets for? "The Shadows of Africa" or "Eight Men in My Wife's Closet"?

SOLOMAN. I accept the challenge.

MICKEY. So what are you going to do with your play?

SOLOMAN. I'll woik on it ... and I'll keep *woiking* till I get it right.

MICKEY. *(Laughs.)* Keep talking like that. Because a black man who talks like that could run for three years at Radio City Music Hall.

(Laughingly, they embrace each other.)

SOLOMAN. I'm going back home to Africa on Saturday. I'll miss you. You've taught me a great deal, Mickey Fox.

MICKEY. God bless you, Soloman Mantutu.... *(The street door opens and RAYLEEN and CHARLES enter. She wears the same coat and hairstyle but her dress is different. CHARLES hasn't changed anything. MICKEY and SOLOMAN see them.)* Wait! You may not get back to Africa for a year.

SOLOMAN. Yes, but I still work here. Excuse me.

(SOLOMAN crosses to them as they stand in the same place they always stand.)

CINDY. *(Also sees RAYLEEN.)* Oh, my god.... What is that

woman wearing?

ARLEEN. I've seen that coat before.... It's from "The Lion King," isn't it?

SOLOMAN. *(To RAYLEEN.)* Good evening.

RAYLEEN. *(Smiles.)* We're two for dinner. My husband Charles and I heard a great deal about your cuisine.

SOLOMAN. *(Smiles.)* Have you? I'm so glad.

RAYLEEN. Charles called for a reservation last night. But the Chinese lady who answered—said you were fully booked.

(SOLOMAN turns to MICKEY. MICKEY mouths "Debby Chang.")

SOLOMAN. Ah yes, Debby Chang. She told me to apologize to you. Her mistake.

RAYLEEN. It's quite alright.... You speak Chinese then?

(SOLOMAN turns to MICKEY. MICKEY shrugs.)

SOLOMAN. Enough to get by with Debby.

RAYLEEN. Can I say hello to her?

SOLOMAN. It's her day off.

RAYLEEN. Well, would you give her a message? *(Insert a Chinese phrase.)*

SOLOMAN. She'll be very grateful.

RAYLEEN. It's such a warm restaurant. The minute you walk in, you feel you've been here before.

SOLOMAN. Others have told me that.

RAYLEEN. And tell me where you're from, dear?

SOLOMAN. South Africa.

RAYLEEN. And you came all the way from South Africa to work in this restaurant. *(To CHARLES.)* No wonder people can't get in here. *(SOLOMAN turns to MICKEY. MICKEY mouths "laugh." SOLOMAN turns back to RAYLEEN and laughs.)* Is anyone special coming tonight? People I would know, that is?

SOLOMAN. Well, it's a house policy not to do that.

RAYLEEN. Alright, give yourself a twenty-dollar tip.... Who's coming?

SOLOMAN. Well ... er ... Mr. Mickey Fox.

RAYLEEN. Mickey Fox? The Senator from Wyoming? Charles and I know him.... Charles, wait till I tell you ....

SOLOMAN. And now, if you would just follow me— *(They walk. We hear a tremendous crash from the kitchen.)* Oh, dear.... One moment, please.

(SOLOMAN rushes off to the kitchen.)

ARLEEN. *(Still looking at CHARLES and RAYLEEN, then to CINDY.)* I have to go home but I want to see what happens next.

RAYLEEN. *(Turns to ARLEEN and CINDY.)* Hello.

ARLEEN. Hello.

RAYLEEN. Dear God, it's Mariana Von Klondishtein.... How are you Mariana? When did you leave Vienna?

ARLEEN. *(Puzzled.)* Vienna?

RAYLEEN. Is this your sister Helga?

ARLEEN. Helga?

(CINDY kicks her under the table.)

CINDY. *(To RAYLEEN.)* Hilga.

RAYLEEN. We'll talk later, yah?

CINDY and ARLEEN. Yah.

(SOLOMAN rushes out, then to MICKEY:)

SOLOMAN. The cook burned his arm badly. I must help him.

(SOLOMAN rushes back into the kitchen.
MICKEY brushes off his sleeves, then in his most dignified manner, crosses to RAYLEEN and CHARLES—the great maitre d'.)

MICKEY. Good evening. How are you? I'm the manager. Are you being helped?

RAYLEEN. *(As if nothing has happened.)* Yes. We made a reservation for dinner. Charles phoned in this afternoon.

MICKEY. Of cawse. Charles. I spoke to him myself. I think we had a bad connection.

RAYLEEN. That was a horrid noise I just heard. We won't be sitting near that, will we?

MICKEY. Oh, no.... That was just the truck delivering the fish.... *(He beckons them to follow him. They do.)* The waiter is getting your tablecloth. It arrived this afternoon from Belgium.

RAYLEEN. Really? We were in Belgium last summer, weren't we, Charles?... Did you hear what I said, Charles?

MICKEY. *(Looks at CHARLES.)* Yes. He looks like he heard it.... Oh, we've already put the tea balls in. They've been dunking them for twenty minutes.

RAYLEEN. Your staff is so clever. But you know that, don't you?

MICKEY. I try.... *(He pulls out chairs for them to sit.)* Now, would you like to hear what our specials are or should we just keep talking about the tea balls for a while?

RAYLEEN. Let's not. I like your style, young man. What is your name again?

MICKEY. Mickey.

RAYLEEN. McGee?

MICKEY. Migel.

RAYLEEN. Miguel?

MICKEY. Yes, Miguel.

RAYLEEN. Miguel, of course.... Charles has some Castilian blood in him but rarely speaks it much these days.

MICKEY. Yes, I thought I noticed that.... By the way, Madame, we're taking all the starch and fats from the tea balls.

RAYLEEN. Your accent, Miguel.... Are you from the island of Las Palmas?

MICKEY. No, but I can see it from my window.... Anything to drink?

RAYLEEN. Do you have a nice Portobello wine in your cellar?

MICKEY. No, but we have some nice Portobello mushrooms growing down there.

RAYLEEN. Oh, bien grathias, Miguel.... Charles! Portobello mushrooms.... Happy now? Oh, Miguel, did you know that Mariana Von Klondishtein and Hilga are here tonight?

MICKEY. Yah?

ARLEEN and CINDY. Yah.

MICKEY and RAYLEEN. Yah.

(MICKEY and RAYLEEN look at CHARLES. BLACKOUT.)

CURTAIN

ACT II

Scene 3
"Winter"

(A cold winter wind blows outside. Taxi's honking, stuck in the snow. There is frosting on the window. BERNIE comes in from outside with a shovel.
BESSIE, an African American, sits playing with her salad.)

BESSIE. How many times are you gonna shovel that snow off, Bernard?

BERNIE. Until someone notices we're open.... Tell me, Bessie, how come you're the only customer who calls me Bernard?

BESSIE. It's your Christian name, isn't it?

BERNIE. Not where I come from.

(ZELDA comes out of kitchen. She is very busy.)

ZELDA. *(To BERNIE.)* Don't just stand there. They say more snow is coming. Every room in the hotel is booked. We're going to run out of food.

BESSIE. Just cut down on the portions. You overfeed them, honey. And raise your prices. This place is the biggest bargain in town.

BERNARD. Good. Tell her.

ZELDA. *(To BESSIE.)* Our customers are kids, actors, people who come in on buses. Bernie and I aren't starving. Our prices are fine.... I'm busy. I got a thousand sandwiches to make....

(ZELDA quickly runs into the kitchen.

MICKEY FOX enters.)

MICKEY. Keep this door locked. A wolf chased me five blocks in the snow. I yelled to the wolf, "Why me? I'm a Fox." He said, "I know. I loved your show." *(He starts to take his coat off.)* Hello, Bessie. I just saw Porgy. He's looking everywhere for you.

BESSIE. Sure wish I was doing "Porgy and Bess." They don't write music like that anymore.

MICKEY. Well, when you're dead, it slows you down a little.

(BERNIE helps him off with his coat.)

BERNIE. Mickey? You got a couple of minutes to give me? It's important.

MICKEY. Sure, sit down.

BERNIE. No. Over there. *(They both cross to the other side, sit on the banquette. Looks around first, then:)* I got a big problem. I sold the restaurant. Zelda doesn't know.

MICKEY. You *SOLD IT?*

BERNIE. Shhh. *(Looks around, then back to him.)* We're getting older. She works too hard. I don't want her to get sick.... SO I bought a condominium in Florida.... This she doesn't know also.... Then yesterday, out of nowhere she says to me, "When we retire one day, I never want to live in Florida."

MICKEY. Now it gets interesting.

BERNIE. I don't know if I can get the restaurant back ... and I don't know if I can sell the condominium.... So what do I tell Zelda?

MICKEY. Dis sounds like a Charles Dickens novel.... Especially with the snow falling.... Let me think a minute, alright, I got it.... You tell the man you sold the restaurant to, that you thought it over and you don't want to sell.... And because he's being so nice, you'll sell him your condo in Florida ... and maybe you'll make a profit. Okay?

BERNIE. It's too late. I signed the papers. He told me a deal is a deal... How do I get out?

MICKEY. Through a window and up to Canada....

(ZELDA comes out.)

ZELDA. *(Snaps at him.)* Bernie, I need you in the kitchen.
BERNIE. I'm coming, Zelda. I'm coming. *(To MICKEY.)* I made a big mistake, didn't I?
MICKEY. She'll forgive you.
BERNIE. You think so?
MICKEY. Not a chance.
ZELDA. *(From kitchen.)* BERNIE!!

(BERNIE runs off to kitchen.)

BESSIE. Everyone's waiting for a call, see if their show is going to cancel tonight.
MICKEY. Cancel is not in my vocabulary. Actually my show is sold out tonight.
BESSIE. Who's coming out to see you on a night like this?
MICKEY. Luckily we found nine hundred Jewish Eskimos. They just called from Connecticut. They stopped to get their snow shoes cleaned.... What do I know. I'm gonna take some beating tonight. *(To BESSIE.)* You're not laughing, Bessie. You don't appreciate sophisticated humor?
BESSIE. And why's that, Mickey? Because I'm a black woman? Do you think we only laugh at the black experience because that's all we understand?
MICKEY. Can you believe this? I survived the coldest night of the century and I walk into a race riot.... Who said anything about black? I've known you eight years, Bessie, this is the foist time I ever noticed it.
BESSIE. Are you going to tell me that's not a racist remark?
MICKEY. Of course it's racist. My whole *act* is racist. If you want to stamp it out you foist bring it out in the open.... You think I'd make a black joke if there wasn't black people in the audience?... I give it to the Jews twice as much. They eat it up.... Well, they'll eat anything up.... I give it to the gentiles, then the Wasps. Only the Wasps think I'm talking about someone else so they don't get it.... I

give it to Asians, Hispanics, Italians.... The Italians don't hear it because they're busy shooting each other in the audience.... But *you* Bessie. Where is this coming from?

BESSIE. I know it's just comedy, honey. I know it's funny. But how come you never talk about the *best* in people?

MICKEY. Who wants to hear about the best in people?... You know what the most successful entertainment was in the year five B.C.? ... Stoning!... Parents would take their kids to a good stoning.... If you threw really big rocks, you could run six years.... You understand?

BESSIE. He who throws the first stone will feel the wrath of God.... Do you know who said that?

MICKEY. Was it you? Because you talk a lot like that.

BESSIE. You're not a religious man, are you?

MICKEY. I'm a practicing Jew, but I haven't hoid if I got in or not.... Bessie, where's your sense of humor?

BESSIE. Read the good book.

MICKEY. I'm waiting for the paperback.... Why are we doing this?

BESSIE. I know humor, honey. 'Cause black folks have been laughing long before Jewish people were smiling.

MICKEY. We didn't have time. We were busy closing up the store.

(MICKEY and BESSIE point at each other because they break each other up. The phone rings. ZELDA gets it at the register but we don't hear her.)

BESSIE. You're funny, man, but you couldn't touch my daddy. No one ever made me laugh like that man.

MICKEY. My father never once laughed at a thing I said. Not once. You know why? He didn't want to give in to me.... But sometimes I'd say something so funny, he'd rush to the bathroom, lock the door and giggle, into a towel.... If it got too loud, he'd shove toilet paper into his mouth.

BESSIE. That's about the saddest thing I ever heard.

MICKEY. I appreciate that, Bessie.... Tell me, how come you

and I never fooled around?

BESSIE. That would be the saddest thing *you* ever heard.

MICKEY. It wasn't for me. I thought *you* might enjoy it.

(BESSIE throws a rolled up napkin at him, it hits the floor. The outside door opens and MEGAN rushes in wearing a cheap parka and hood, scarf and her bag of plays.)

MEGAN. *(Panting.)* Wow, this is so great. Snow in New York. Isn't it romantic?

MICKEY. Only if you're in love with empty theaters.

MEGAN. Hi, Mr. Fox. Hi, Bessie. *(To ZELDA.)* Sorry I'm late, Zelda. *(She picks up napkin from the floor. To MICKEY and BESSIE.)* Is there anything I can get you? Coffee? Tea?

MICKEY. You woiking here now?

MEGAN. Part-time. I lost my other job. I was spending too much time in acting class.

ZELDA. *(Hangs up phone.)* They're starting to order from upstairs. You'll have to make a few deliveries.

MEGAN. Absolutely.

MICKEY. Who are you studying with?

MEGAN. Sascha Dubrinski.... Do you know him?

MICKEY. Sure. He was a lousy actor so he toined to teaching.... You like him?

MEGAN. Well, he doesn't really teach. He has someone else teach. And you don't know what he thinks because he only talks to the teacher.... Is that what they call "The Method"?

MICKEY. No, that's what they call "faking it."

MEGAN. Who did you study with?

MICKEY. My older brother, Harry. He had no humor. If I could just keep him awake, I knew I'd be a smash hit.

ZELDA. Megan, are you working for me or not?

MEGAN. You bet, Zelda. I love this place. It's like a great school with terrific sandwiches.

(MEGAN goes.)

BERNIE. *(Comes out.)* Mickey. Your brother called. Said he'll be a few minutes late.

MICKEY. Good. An hour late would be better. Never would be poifect.

(BERNIE goes back inside. MICKEY sees BESSIE.)

BERNIE. You got a problem with him?

MICKEY. Like everyone. It's a sibling rivalry.

BESSIE. I got that with my sister.

MICKEY. *(To BESSIE.)* Good. Then let's exchange sibbles.... See if you get along with a short Jewish older man with no humor who asks for favors all the time.... And what's your sister like?

BESSIE. Same thing. Only she ain't Jewish, she ain't older, she's got humor and she don't ask for favors.

MICKEY. So what don't you like about her?

BESSIE. That she's my sister.

BERNIE. Mickey, should I make anything special for your brother?

MICKEY. Yeah. Something to take out.... It's not a poifect relationship.... I'm going to the men's room. Not because I have to go, but I have to figure out how I'm going to say no to him for the twenty-foist time.... He means well. I just wish he'd mean well to someone else.

(MICKEY's about to leave when BERNIE calls out.)

BERNIE. Mickey!

(He gestures with his head to indicate ZELDA.)

MICKEY. Oh, Zelda.

ZELDA. Yes?

MICKEY. Christmas is coming soon. I've rented a condominium in Florida for you and Bernie for the holidays.... What do you say?

ZELDA. That's very sweet of you, Mickey.... Bernie would love it. I hate Florida.

BERNIE. Why? Poifect weather. Sandy beaches. Why don't you like it?

ZELDA. People go there to retire. I don't want to retire.... Ever.

MICKEY. Funny, I can't wait to retire.... I'm tired of being booked all the time.... In Florida I would sleep late, then get up and take a nap ... then a massage, then forty winks, another massage, then I'd be so tired from the naps and massages, I'd go to bed early.... You'd love it.

ZELDA. Not for me.... Work is what keeps me young.

MICKEY. Then you're in the wrong place. The Fountain of Youth is in Florida.... My father lives there now. He'll be thirty-six in August.

ZELDA. I'm better off here, Mickey.... I'll be twenty-eight in June.

(ZELDA goes off.)

MICKEY. *(Aloud to himself.)* Oh, Boinie, you're in such trouble.

(MICKEY goes off to bathroom. MEGAN comes out, coat off, with a list and a pencil.... She crosses to BESSIE.)

MEGAN. Bessie? Could I talk to you? It's really important.

BESSIE. If it's important, you've come to the right place. What is it, honey?

MEGAN. Well.... I just don't think I can cut it.... This acting thing.... I shake every time I get up in front of the class.... My heart pounds, my knees wobble and you can't hear me three feet away.... I get very big laughs but it's usually in a dramatic scene. To tell you the truth, I want to pack up and go home tonight.

BESSIE. Nobody said it was easy.

MEGAN. I know. But nobody told me that nobody said it was easy.... My mother told me she loved every minute of it even though nobody told her she was any good.... She still does amateur plays in Ohio and everyone tells her she's wonderful ... but I think she's just an amateur.... She just loves the getting up in front of people part....

And I'm beginning to think I inherited her lack of talent.

BESSIE. So what's your question?

MEGAN. When did you know you were really good?

BESSIE. Never!... You must never think you're really good, honey. You've got to *always* be in the developing stage.... *Always* learning, always honing your craft, right up to the time you retire.... 'Cause the minute you think you're really good, you stop growing.... You get self-satisfied and audiences don't like that. They're smart.... They say, "Who does that girl think she is? I'm paying a lot of money for this seat. I'm not getting my money's worth of acting from that woman. She's self-satisfied, that's what she is.... Get somebody in that part who's gonna take chances, risk everything, surprise me, frighten me, fall flat on your face for me but don't stand up there showing me that self-satisfied smugness because you think you're really good.... Hell, woman, if you can't do that, I'll go up there and do the part *for* you.... You hear me?" ... You understand what I'm saying, Megan?

MEGAN. Yes. Wow!... That was really good, Bessie.... When did you learn that?

BESSIE. Just now. I made it up as I went along.... It was pretty good but not *really* good.

(They both laugh.)

MEGAN. Bessie, you are just about the most—

BESSIE. Don't get all sentimental with me, Megan. I've seen too many Mammy movies that ended like this.

MEGAN. *(Nods, smiles.)* Okay. I got it.

(MEGAN turns and goes.
BERNIE comes out.)

BERNIE. MEGAN!!

MEGAN. I'm coming, Zelda. I'm coming!

(MEGAN goes.

The outside door opens. HARRY, Mickey's brother, enters. About two years older than MICKEY. He walks and talks like MICKEY, and also dresses like him.)

BERNIE. Can I help you?
HARRY. Why not? I'm Harry Fox. Mickey Fox's brother. You hoid of him, I'm sure.
BERNIE. Yes, of course. He'll be right back.
HARRY. I know where he went. Whenever I meet him somewhere, that's where he runs to.... He did it since he was five.
BERNIE. Well, would you like to sit? This is his table.
HARRY. *(Takes off his coat.)* I expected a bigger place. Everybody in Philadelphia hoid of the Polish Tea Room.
BERNIE. They do? I wonder why?
HARRY. Good woid of mouth. It's essential for a restaurant. I own a stationery store. It's hard for a stationery store to get good woid of mouth.... That wasn't a joke. I'm not the funny one. You can tell, right?
BERNIE. *(Smiles, nods.)* Can I get you anything while you wait?
HARRY. I don't know how long I'll be here. It depends on his mood.... I talk like him, don't I?
BERNIE. Yes.
HARRY. He got that from me. I'm two years older.

(BERNIE turns, MICKEY enters.)

MICKEY. Harry! Nobody told me you were here.
HARRY. Because nobody else had to go to the toilet.
MICKEY. *(Gives him a perfunctory hug.)* Nice seeing you, Harry. You're looking very good.
HARRY. Why not? I'm wearing your suit ... *and* your coat. The hat is mine. *(They sit.)* I keep feeling in the pockets. Maybe you left a showgirl's phone number for me.
MICKEY. I didn't know you wanted one.
HARRY. I don't. I just wanted to know what it felt like.
MICKEY. *(Laughs a little.)* And how's your wife?

HARRY. Her name is Lenore.

MICKEY. I didn't forget it, Harry. I'm sorry.

HARRY. It was a joke, I don't make them good.... She's fine. She had a tuck.

MICKEY. A what?

HARRY. A tuck.

MICKEY. A tuck?

HARRY. Under the neck. A sixty-year-old woman with a twenty-eight-year-old neck.... She threw away all her turtleneck sweaters. *(MICKEY laughs.)* ... Listen, Mickey. I want to thank you for taking the time out of your busy life to see me.

MICKEY. Harry, stop it.

HARRY. What'd I say? You're a busy man. You've been a busy man since you were twelve years old.

MICKEY. Okay. Fine.... And how's Philadelphia?

HARRY. I don't know. I didn't read the paper today. Remember you used to say that? Momma would ask you, "Mickey, you feeling alright?" and you'd say, "I don't know. I didn't read the paper today." *(He laughs.)* You remember?

MICKEY. I don't remember everything I said, Harry.

HARRY. I do. Every woid you ever said.

MICKEY. Thank you. And how's the shop?

HARRY. It's a stationery store, not a shop. It's not a fancy place. I sell paperclips.

MICKEY. Harry, you've squeezed three innuendos in three sentences.... You must be hungry. I'll buy you dinner.

HARRY. How do you know? Maybe *I'll* buy dinner. It's possible.

MICKEY. Alright. *Four* innuendos.

(ZELDA comes over.)

ZELDA. Mickey? Is this your brother?

MICKEY. Yes. Zelda, this is Harry, my brother from Philadelphia.

ZELDA. Philadelphia. The birthplace of America, right?

HARRY. Right. I forget the hospital.... That's Mickey's joke. He did it in a school show.... Fourteen years old, I knew even then he was going to be a big star.

ZELDA. You must be very proud.

HARRY. Why not? It's good for business. Everybody calls my place Mickey Fox's Brother's Stationery Store.

MICKEY. *(Wants to move on.)* Could we have two teas, Zelda?

ZELDA. Whatever you want.... Very nice to meet you, Harry.

HARRY. Thank you. The pleasure is ours. *(Pointing to himself and MICKEY. He laughs, ZELDA smiles and leaves.)* Remember when you foist said that, Mickey?

MICKEY. Harry, are you going to go through my entire Hit Parade of talking?

HARRY. I said something wrong? You always look at me like I embarrassed you.

MICKEY. You're my big brother, Harry. I don't make judgments about you.

HARRY. I know. You don't make phone calls either. *(MICKEY looks away.)* Alright, that was a wrong thing to say. I apologize. Does this mean you're going to the bathroom again?

MICKEY. Harry, can't we just once ...?

HARRY. I don't think so.

MICKEY. You didn't even wait till I finished.

HARRY. Alright. Finish.

MICKEY. Never mind. It's not important.

HARRY. So why are you angry that I didn't let you finish?

(BERNIE comes out.)

BERNIE. Bessie? Your stage manager just called. They canceled tonight's show.

BESSIE. I figured. One last cup of coffee, Bernie.

BERNIE. Mickey? Should I call your theater?

MICKEY. I'm not canceling. No matter what. Tell them to go out and find poor people and fill up the theater with them.

BERNIE. That's a nice gesture, Mickey.

MICKEY. And they'll pay whatever they can. *(HARRY looks at him.)* It's a joke, Harry.... I was not serious.

HARRY. I know that. Still it was a generous offer.

BESSIE. Mickey! This would have been a *gooooood* night to walk me home.

HARRY. What's that about??

MICKEY. Nothing, Harry. She was just kidding.

HARRY. I know that. Still it was a generous offer.

MICKEY. So. I suppose we're going to talk about the same subject again, right?

HARRY. Not if you don't want to.

MICKEY. The truth? I really don't, Harry.

HARRY. Then forget it. I won't bother you.... Is it alright if *I* talk about it and you just listen?

MICKEY. *(Doesn't want to push it.)* Alright. Thank you. It's a generous offer, Harry.

HARRY. Steven is good, Mickey. Not as good as you, of course, but he's good. Not just because he's my son, but I think he has something. *(Reaches into pocket.)* I brought his reviews. I want you to read them.

MICKEY. I read them for five years in a row, Harry. They never get better.

HARRY. I know. But they never get woise either.... Look at this one. From Trenton, New Jersey. "Coming next week, rising young comic Steven Fox."

MICKEY. That's not a review, Harry. It's an announcement that he's coming to Trenton, New Jersey....

HARRY. *Rising* young comic?

MICKEY. We don't know how far down he came from.... And every comic sends that in. "Rising young comic.... Hilarious young comic.... Brilliant young comic." ... I did that when I was seventeen.... I sent my résumé and picture to a club and signed it, "Phenomenal Mickey Fox." ... I got booked in for one night and the owner comes over and says, "Who told you you were phenomenal?" And I said, "No one. That's my first name. Phenomenal." ... We lie, Harry.

HARRY. I'm not asking you to come see him. I'll have him come to your apartment and do his act for you.

MICKEY. Oy gut... I'm tired when I come home. I fall asleep in ten minutes.

HARRY. He can do his act in six minutes.

MICKEY. Sometimes I fall asleep when I hit the pillow.

HARRY. He can start while you're putting on your pajamas.

MICKEY. Stop pushing, Harry.

HARRY. I HAVE TO PUSH!! THAT'S WHAT A FATHER DOES FOR HIS SON.... I'm sorry. I didn't mean to shout.

MICKEY. Harry, he's forty-one years old.... You don't start to be a comic when you're forty-one.... That's a very young audience out there. He's a beginner. He has no experience.... Maybe you can book him on a cruise. He can make animal balloons for kids.

HARRY. You were funny at twelve and you had no experience.

MICKEY. I didn't even know I was funny. I said the truth and everyone laughed.... At dinner I would say, "Momma, can I have a hammer for the matzoh balls." It wasn't a joke. I meant it... She cooked everything hard.... You couldn't chop her chopped liver.... Life is funny, Harry. Not jokes. Does Steven know that?

HARRY. You could tell him.

MICKEY. *You* tell him. Life is funny. Not jokes. Tell him.

HARRY. You tell it funnier. That's why you have your own table here.

MICKEY. What does he want this for? Tell him to be a lawyer.

HARRY. He is.

MICKEY. I know he is. But I couldn't do that. Being a lawyer takes intelligence. I'm stuck with being funny.

HARRY. He's willing to give up his law practice. That's how much he wants it.

MICKEY. Maybe he could become a funny lawyer. They're very hard to find.

HARRY. It took him four years to pass the bar. He's my son, Mickey, but he's not that good a lawyer. He handles five and ten dollar cases.... A man fell in my store. He sued for ten thousand dollars. I gave Steven the case. He lost, the man got *thirty* thousand.... He hasn't got his heart in it. He went to law school because I made him. I *forced* him to go ... and I made a mistake. He wants to make people laugh.... When the man got thirty thousand dollars, he laughed ... and that made Steven feel good.

MICKEY. Does he make you laugh, Harry?

HARRY. No. He makes me cry. Because I think I ruined his life.

MICKEY. *(Sighs.)* Ohh, Harry, don't you understand? Being funny isn't a job. It isn't even a talent. It's a *curse*. A comic doesn't leave life alone.... He pushes it and nudges it until he can squeeze a laugh out of it. And eventually that's all his life is.... You can't even keep a marriage going because you're too busy looking for a topic, a subject, a target, a premise, a sound, a noise, a face, a walk, a prayer to God that maybe they'll like you and not just stare at you because you're standing up there stark naked without anything to cover up your shame and humiliation because you're just not FUCKING FUNNY.... Do you know what the Mona Lisa is when there's no one in the museum? It's still a great piece of art.... Do you know what a comic is with an audience who looks at you like they wished you'd go home? You're a waste of their time.... Better a lousy lawyer, Harry, then to rob someone of their time and their attention.

HARRY. I know but will you help him, Mickey?

MICKEY. *(Frustrated.)* Why?

HARRY. Because you owe it to him.

MICKEY. For what?

HARRY. For being a better example to him than I was.... He idolizes you. Me he tolerates.

MICKEY. Why are you so hard on yourself, Harry?

HARRY. Why not? What did I ever do with my life?

MICKEY. Please, let's not toin this into "It's a Wonderful Life." ... I haven't got time to show you what the woild would have been without you.... You know what doesn't woik *on* stage and *off* stage, Harry?

HARRY. What?

MICKEY. Self-pity.

HARRY. I don't pity me. Other people do.

MICKEY. I've had walnuts, Brazil nuts, macadamia nuts and coconuts, but you are the hardest nut to crack in the woild, Harry....

You've had that stationery store for thirty-eight years, and it's still doing business. People must like you.

HARRY. They do. Friends I keep. Family is harder. Lenore blames me for what's happening to Steven. That I pushed him too hard.... And now I think I'm losing Lenore too.

MICKEY. Well, look at it dis way. If you break up, Steven can handle the divorce.... I'm sorry. See what I mean? Comics are bloodsuckers.... Let me think a minute.

(MICKEY gets up.)

HARRY. You're going to the toilet again? You can't escape life in the toilet.

MICKEY. I know. But there's something about our relationship that my bladder can't handle.... Don't go away.

(MICKEY heads for the lobby. HARRY looks at BESSIE.)

HARRY. I'm Mickey Fox's brother, Harry Fox.

BESSIE. Oh, yes. You own that stationery story in Philadelphia.

HARRY. You hoid of it?

BESSIE. Oh, sure. It's got good word of mouth.

HARRY. *(Smiles.)* You in show business too?

BESSIE. *(Nods.)* Mm hmm.

HARRY. I bet you're really good.

BESSIE. Yes, I am.

(As BESSIE leaves, ARLEEN and CINDY come in from the street door. ARLEEN is talking into a cell phone.)

ARLEEN. ... our car is in the parking lot, frozen stiff. It won't start. And if it did, it couldn't get out anyway.

CINDY. *(To MEGAN.)* Can we get a table, please?

MEGAN. Anywhere you want.

CINDY. Is Soloman here? Soloman Mantutu?

MEGAN. No. Sorry. He went back to South Africa months ago.

CINDY. Too bad. *(The two women follow MEGAN to a table. As they sit, to MEGAN.)* Well, he recommended the blintzes so that's what we'll have. And two teas.

(MEGAN smiles, nods and goes back to the kitchen.)

ARLEEN. *(Into cell phone.)* Jack, can you still hear me?... Okay, so we went to a backers' audition. You know, for a new play? They're asking money for this show.... You crazy? I'd never invest. But we got to see it free.... I don't know. I'll ask. *(To CINDY.)* Where'd they get our names?

CINDY. They have the names of every person who ever bought a ticket by phone or mail.... It's like Big Brother.

ARLEEN. *(Into phone.)* Did you hear that?... You want to hear how bad it was?... It was the only show that closed at a backers' audition.

CINDY. Tell him there were twenty-one producers.

ARLEEN. *(Into phone.)* This show had twenty-one producers.... And after the intermission, there were eight producers.

CINDY. Tell him about the little old lady who left early, then slipped in the snow.

ARLEEN. *(Into phone.)* Oh, right. A little old lady left early and slipped in the snow ... and she refused to be carried back in.

CINDY. Can I speak to him a second? *(She takes the phone out of ARLEEN's hand, then into phone.)* Jack? Listen to this.... It's a musical about the life of Irving Berlin. Only the Irving Berlin estate won't let them use any of his songs.... So they got a composer who wrote songs that *sounded* like Irving Berlin.

ARLEEN. Let me speak to him. *(She takes the phone back.)* So this guy brings up what it's going to cost. He says, "We can bring this into Broadway for eight million dollars, *or*, we can do it *Off* Broadway for a million and a half." ... And this woman says, "Isn't it better to lose a million and a half than eight million?"

CINDY. *(Grabs the phone away.)* And this was the wife of the producer.

(CINDY gives the phone back to ARLEEN.)

ARLEEN. *(Into phone.)* And when this guy is finished talking, *another* producer grabs the mike and says, "For those who want to stay, we have an *alternate* musical to show you."

CINDY. *(Motions with fingers for the phone. ARLEEN gives it to her.... Into the phone.)* Listen to this. All the producers were German, Scandinavian or Dutch. And they said, "If you invest twenty thousand dollars, you get a free trip to their country." ... And some woman gets up and says, "How much is the trip without the investment?"

(CINDY gives phone back to ARLEEN.)

ARLEEN. *(Into phone.)* And then, out of nowhere, the producers got into a huge fistfight.... I mean they were punching the shit out of each other.... There was blood everywhere, they called the cops.... But everyone in the audience stayed for the entire fight ... and gave it a standing ovation.

(CINDY laughs hysterically.)

CINDY. *(Yells into phone.)* Actually, it was the best thing we saw this season.

ARLEEN. *(Into the phone.)* No more plays for us.... We're only going to backers' auditions.... See you at home.

(They hang up, sit, laughing.
MICKEY walks back in, sits opposite HARRY.)

HARRY. *(To MICKEY.)* Maybe I can get Steven into a backers' audition.

MICKEY. If I did help Steven when would I do it? I woik six days a week.

HARRY. If you could just give him an hour a day.

MICKEY. Harry, at my age, an hour a day is the last two years of my life.

HARRY. A *half* hour. And if not every day, whenever you can.

MICKEY. I'm not a teacher, Harry. I woik by instinct. You can't teach instinct. If you could, there would be comics all over Broadway instincting up the place.

HARRY. See! Like that. He would pick up things like that. Like a baby learns to speak by listening to its parents.

(The outside door opens and RAYLEEN and CHARLES come in. She is wearing her usual coat but with a Russian fur hat and white leather boots. CHARLES wears his suit but he wears earmuffs and a New York Knicks woolen jacket over it. They stand there.)

MICKEY. *(Looks up and sees them.)* Poifect! Look who walks in here.... Harry, can you look without turning around?

HARRY. *(Tries but can't.)* My neck doesn't turn anymore anyway.

MICKEY. Alright, move your chair a little. *(HARRY moves his chair a little, sees them.)* Zelda, customers.

HARRY. So?

MICKEY. What do you think of that couple?

HARRY. *(Squints.)* I don't know. I think she has a lousy dry cleaner.

MICKEY. Put Steven in dis restaurant five days a week, he doesn't have to loin from me.

(MEGAN crosses out, sees RAYLEEN, crosses to them.)

MEGAN. Hello. May I help you?

RAYLEEN. Oh, bless you, child. Do you recognize us? Mr. and Mrs. Charles W. Browning the third?

MEGAN. Oh, yes, Mrs. Browning.

RAYLEEN. The third.

MEGAN. Oh, yes, Mrs. Browning the third.... I remember your coat. It's very unusual.

RAYLEEN. Oh, thank you dear. It was my design. It started off as a bolero jacket and each year it just seemed to grow.... I have another one at home. It's blue but I think it's a bit much.

MEGAN. Can I show you to a table?

RAYLEEN. Well, to be brutally honest, we don't have a reservation. We were just passing by and I thought, let's try it, Charles.

MEGAN. Fine. Just follow me.

(They do. They pass MICKEY. RAYLEEN slows to speak to MICKEY.)

RAYLEEN. *(To MICKEY.)* Miguel!!... You're back from Las Palmas.

MICKEY. Yes. I noticed that myself.... I came back. I missed the snow.

RAYLEEN. No, you didn't. It's all over the place.... Charles and I used to ski at night in St. Moritz ... by torchlight.

MICKEY. I did too but they made me stop.... I burned down too many trees.

RAYLEEN. Have you lost your accent?

MICKEY. I think so. I forget what it was.

RAYLEEN. You're so droll.... You don't meet droll people anymore.... Where did all the droll people go?

MICKEY. I don't know. Ask Charles.

RAYLEEN. He can't order from the menu, how would he know where all the droll people went?... Didn't you have a chalet in St. Moritz?

MICKEY. No, I had a valet in Las Palmas.

RAYLEEN. Well, you must know that Charles and I lost our chalet in St. Moritz. Burned down.... You can't depend on him to yell "Fire." ... Call me. It's the same number.

(RAYLEEN goes off with CHARLES.)

HARRY. *(To MICKEY.)* You have a chalet?

MICKEY. If I tried to explain all this, none of us would live long enough.

(ZELDA comes out and crosses to RAYLEEN.)

ZELDA. I'm surprised to see you out in this weather.

RAYLEEN. Well, Charles just adores it. His family had a dacha in Moscow. The wonderful thing about living so far north is that you get your Christmas presents so early.... Didn't they, Charles?... Well, once he starts reminiscing, you can't stop him.

(They are seated.)

ZELDA. Did you want to start off with your two kinds of hot tea?

RAYLEEN. Tea? No. We rarely drink tea. It can cause terrible gastric distress.... Charles is the expert. Tell her, dear.

(She looks at the menu. CHARLES says nothing.)

ZELDA. We're expecting the place to be filled up in about ten minutes, so if you could place your order soon....

RAYLEEN. Well, Charles knows what he wants. I'm the dawdler.... *(Looks at menu.)* Dawdle dawdle dawdle.... How is the Pacific sea bass?

ZELDA. In the Pacific. We don't make it. It's not on the menu.

RAYLEEN. Then don't worry yourself. I'll have a chiliburger and fries.... Is it yum yum?

ZELDA. It's very yum yum.... Thank you. *(She takes the menu and goes. As she passes MICKEY.)* I wonder if she wants me to feed the coat too.

RAYLEEN. *(To CHARLES.)* I know what you're doing, Charles. You're thinking in French again, aren't you?.... You've been doing that an awful lot lately and I don't like it.

HARRY. *(Aside to MICKEY.)* Doesn't he talk?

MICKEY. Who knows if he's alive?... Tell me something, Harry. If I had a forty-one-year-old daughter who was a doctor, and she wanted to quit to woik in a stationery store, what would you say to her?

HARRY. *(Looks at him.)* Do you have a daughter?

MICKEY. No.

HARRY. Is she a doctor?

MICKEY. No.

HARRY. So why do you make up a story that's not in this equation?... I knew I was wasting my time coming here. Lenore said don't go to him. He's not the kind who does favors.... As usual, Lenore was right.

(HARRY gets up, reaches for his coat.

MICKEY. Harry. Sit down. We're not through with this yet. Alright? *(HARRY sits, looks at him.)* ... You sent me a tape of Steven's woik two, three year ago. Right?

HARRY. Right. I called you, you said he has possibilities. Am I lying?

MICKEY. No, Harry, *I* was lying. I did *not* think he had possibilities. I was being polite ... but I'll do what you want. I'll woik with him, an hour here, and hour there, whatever.... But I'm not doing it for him, Harry. I'm doing it for *you*.... Is that what you want?

HARRY. No. I want you to do it for him.

MICKEY. I see.... You know what I think, Harry? I think you're testing me. I think you're asking me if I love you enough.

HARRY. I don't give a damn what you think it's about. I'm asking you to help my son. Leave you and me out of this, God dammit.... I'll never ask you for anything again in my entire life, I swear to God. *(He gets up.)* Except one thing. Where's the toilet? Now it's *my* toin to go.

(HARRY starts to go.)

MICKEY. It's out in the—

HARRY. NEVER MIND! I'LL FIND IT MYSELF.

(HARRY storms out.)

RAYLEEN. *(Looking around.)* Have I overrated this restaurant, Charles?... I thought *you* might like it but God knows what you like. *(CHARLES rubs his temples.)* Another migraine? You can stop it now if you'd only do what I tell you.... But you won't. You never do....

You really love your migraines, don't you? *(He rubs them harder. She turns, looks at MICKEY a little flirtatiously.)* So tell me, Miguel, how is the love of your life? What was her name again? Refresh me.

MICKEY. Er ... Guadalupay.

RAYLEEN. Guadalupay? I thought it was Genvieve.

MICKEY. Oh. Yes.... Sad story ... Genvieve — est morte.

RAYLEEN. *(Looks at him.)* Genvieve is going with Mort?

MICKEY. No. Genvieve is dead. At least the marriage is dead.

RAYLEEN. And Mort?

MICKEY. Mort is really dead.

RAYLEEN. How sad. I liked Genvieve.... And where did you meet Guadalupay?

MICKEY. In — Guadalcanal.... I went there on a cruise.

RAYLEEN. No, I can't say I've been to Guadalcanal. Sounds horrid. What was the food like?

MICKEY. Spam, mostly....

RAYLEEN. You're tweaking me, aren't you?... You're a tweaker, I can tell.... Well, if ever I'm in Guadalcanal, I'll look up Guadalupay. *(She smiles, then turns back to CHARLES. Aside to CHARLES.)* The man is a deadbeat, Charles.

(HARRY comes back, picks up his coat and starts to put it on.)

ARLEEN. I miss Mantutu. Do you?

CINDY. I do. I miss Mantutu, too.

MICKEY. Harry, listen to me—

HARRY. NO! You listen to *me*.... I tremble every time I come to see you ... because I'm afraid I'll say what I really feel.... I don't mind living in your shadow ... but I don't have a shadow of my own ... not on the sunniest day.... I can buy my own suits, I don't need yours.... I wear them because when people say, "Are you really Mickey Fox's brother?" I tell them, "This is his suit I'm wearing." ... Even my own suits don't have a shadow ... other people can come right up and ask for your autograph.... And I'm afraid to ask for a favor.... But still I love you.... And if I didn't have you, I could have a shadow a mile long, but I wouldn't have you, my kid brother.... I'm sorry. Forgive me.

MICKEY. ... Harry! Tell Steven we start woiking next week. Now sit down and we'll have dinner.

HARRY. *(Stops, looks at him.)* No conditions?

MICKEY. One. Sit on this side. I don't want you to be in my shadow.

HARRY. It's alright. I'd miss it. *(MICKEY nods and HARRY sits down.)* So I'm finally gonna eat in the Polish Tea Room.

(HARRY picks up the menu.)

RAYLEEN. Leave your head alone, Charles. You can have your migraine for dessert.... Did you decide what you wanted to eat?... Tell me, Charles.

CHARLES. ... One....

RAYLEEN. One? One what, Charles? *(She looks at menu.)*

CHARLES. One ... one d....

RAYLEEN. Yes, I heard, Charles. One what?... Do you mean number one on the menu? *(She looks at menu.)* The turkey hot plate? No, I don't think you'd care for that, Charles.

CHARLES. One day.... One day you will —

RAYLEEN. You're repeating yourself, dear.... What did Mommy tell you about repeating yourself?

CHARLES. One day you will never see me again.

RAYLEEN. Yes, Charles, I know.... You've told me that many times....

CHARLES. One day I'll never hear your voice again.... One day you'll stop telling me what to do....

RAYLEEN. Of course, dear. Oh look, Charles, they have Russian borscht.... You've *always* loved Russian borscht, haven't you....

CHARLES. *(Cue after RAYLEEN's "Of course, dear," getting louder.)* I'm sick of taking care of you....

RAYLEEN. Are you? I thought you enjoyed it, dear.

CHARLES. *(He starts to rise halfway out of chair.)* I'm sick of watching over you.... I'm sick of being a NURSE to you.

RAYLEEN. I'm going to have apple pie.

CHARLES. *(He stands over her now.)* I'm sick of dressing you and undressing you.... I'm sick of running your baths and washing your back.

RAYLEEN. *(Turns and smiles at MICKEY.)* Charles loves to make speeches.... He was almost Governor of North Carolina, you know.

CHARLES. You would die without me, you know you will.... You would die in your bed if I didn't help you out in the morning....

RAYLEEN. *(To MICKEY.)* His mother was almost a Duchess in England....

CHARLES. You couldn't live another day if I weren't there to get you through your miserable life.... YOU KNOW THAT DON'T YOU. Don't you.

RAYLEEN. Yes, Charles, I know that.

CHARLES. I'm sorry. I'm so sorry.

RAYLEEN. *(Strokes CHARLES' head.)* That's my Charley boy.... All tired out now, aren't you.... Mother will find something sweet for you.... A pudding, perhaps.... Does Charles W. Browning the third want some marvelously wonderful lemon custard ... eh, Charley?

(MICKEY and HARRY look at each other.
DIMOUT.)

Scene 4
"Spring"

(A warm day in May. ANDREW DUNCAN sits alone at MICKEY's table.
ARLEEN and CINDY sit at a table on the other side of the room. Their dialogue should move quickly.)

CINDY. What's wrong? Something's bothering you, I can tell.

ARLEEN. I don't want to talk about it.

CINDY. It's the play we saw today. It depressed you. It depressed *everyone*. It was lousy. Is that it?

ARLEEN. In a sense, yes.

CINDY. It's just a rotten play. Forget about it.

ARLEEN. I can't.

CINDY. Why not?

ARLEEN. I invested in it.

CINDY. *WHAT??? ARE YOU CRAZY???*

ARLEEN. Will you lower your voice? You want my husband to find out?

CINDY. Jack doesn't know???

ARLEEN. You think I told him? I'm crazy but not that crazy.

CINDY. How much did you put in?

ARLEEN. I don't want to talk about it.

CINDY. More than a thousand?.... More than five thousand?

ARLEEN. I don't want to talk about it.

CINDY. More than *ten* thousand?

ARLEEN. What's a good hotel in this area? I'm moving out before he comes home.

(ZELDA is behind the cash register, BERNIE comes in. He takes her aside.)

BERNIE. Zelda, I can't keep it in anymore. I can't sleep, I can't breathe, I can't eat a thing.

ZELDA. Maybe you should eat somewhere else than here.... What's wrong?

BERNIE. Don't hate me.... I sold the restaurant. *(She looks at him, shocked.)* We got a very good price. More than I expected.

ZELDA. I don't believe it.

BERNIE. Believe it.

ZELDA. Without asking me? Why would you do that?

BERNIE. You work too hard. I didn't want you to get sick. I bought us a condominium in Florida.

ZELDA. In *Florida*??? Did Mickey put you up to this?

BERNIE. No, I swear to God.

ZELDA. Well, cancel the sale. We're not moving.

BERNIE. I can't. The man said a deal is a deal.

ZELDA. Who is this man?

BERNIE. I forget his name. I dealt with his lawyers. They want to close in three weeks.

ZELDA. We'll see.... It'll come out the way it should come out.... Don't worry. Don't get sick.... Don't tell anyone about this yet.

BERNIE. I haven't, I swear.

ZELDA. We made a lot of friends here. They'd miss this place. We all would.

BERNIE. My mouth is shut.

ZELDA. Good. I got people waiting.

BERNIE. Then you're not angry with me?

ZELDA. Of *course* I'm angry with you. After all these years you don't ASK me first? Are we husband and wife? Are we partners? Didn't we grow up together? Isn't my pillow next to *your* pillow? Are my children *your* children?... I am angry and I'm furious.... *(Letting up.)* But I'll get over it. Don't worry. *(Pats his cheek with her hand.)* Just figure out how we're going to get the restaurant back, sweetheart. *(She smiles at him, crosses to ANDREW.)* Can I get you anything, Mr. Duncan?

ANDREW. No, thank you very much.... How is it you make better tea than they do in England?

ZELDA. I don't use English tea.

(BESSIE comes in, sits down at a table.)

CINDY. Did you read the play before you invested?

ARLEEN. A couple of pages.

CINDY. That's all? And you invested?

ARLEEN. I liked the title.

CINDY. "My Father Was a Grape"?? ... You invested in "My Father Was a Grape"?? ... What does it mean?

ARLEEN. I though it meant something else. I didn't know it really meant a grape.

(ZELDA crosses to BESSIE.)

ZELDA. So, Bessie, what's new?

BESSIE. I heard you and Bernie were selling this place.

ZELDA. *(Shocked.)* Where did you hear such a crazy thing?

BESSIE. It's all up and down the street. Maybe Bernie didn't tell you.

ZELDA. Bernie tells me everything.

BESSIE. You know what my advice is?

ZELDA. What?

BESSIE. Whatever they offer, you ask for more. It ain't the restaurant that brings people in here. It's you and Bernard. Without you two, this place is just a bunch of tables looking for someone to sit in.

ZELDA. Well, in the first place, we're not selling. And in the second place, this is something Bernie and I should talk about right away. *(ZELDA crosses. BERNIE is on the phone at the register. ZELDA motions for BERNIE to get off the phone. He hangs up.)* How did Bessie know? She heard about it.

BERNIE. Not from me, I swear. I told nobody.... What did she say?

ZELDA. She said we should get more money.

BERNIE. I didn't even tell you what they offered.

ZELDA. I don't care. It should be more.... I have work to do.

(ZELDA walks away leaving BERNIE bewildered.
MICKEY comes in, sees BESSIE.)

CINDY. I don't understand. They didn't even have grapes in the show.

ARLEEN. Did they have an elephant in "The Elephant Man"?

MICKEY. I just came from the doctor. A three-hour examination. They don't know what caused it.

BESSIE. Caused what?

MICKEY. I woke up this morning and I wasn't funny. Andrew, don't go back to England. I'll be right there. *(To BESSIE.)* I gotta hunch he's gonna offer me the "Vagina Monologues."

BESSIE. Did you hear about Bernie and Zelda?

MICKEY. Yeah. They're selling the restaurant.

BESSIE. Who told you?

MICKEY. Bernie.

BESSIE. Then it's true?

MICKEY. Maybe not. When a man Bernie's age wakes up in the morning, he feels he has to sell something.

(MEGAN comes out.)

MEGAN. Got your sandwich, Bessie, tuna to go.... Hi, Mr. Fox. What's new?

MICKEY. Aside from my show closing next week, nothing.

MEGAN. *It's closing??*

MICKEY. It was a limited engagement. When they stop coming, I limit the engagement.

ARLEEN. *(Waves to MEGAN.)* Oh, miss ....

BESSIE. *(To MICKEY.)* Well, don't tell anyone else about the closing.

MICKEY. Who would I tell?

(MICKEY crosses to ANDREW. ANDREW stands.)

ANDREW. Mickey! So good to see you again.

MICKEY. Bernie and Zelda are closing the restaurant.

ANDREW. It's closing?

MICKEY. Don't say anything. Nobody knows this but me, Bessie, Bernie, Zelda, a few other people I told and now you.

ANDREW. I hope not. Every day the world loses a little more charm than it can afford.

MICKEY. Well, you're looking terrific. *(ANDREW laughs.)* Are we finally going to woik together?

ANDREW. Well, to that I say Here Here.

MICKEY. Or There There, wherever you want.

(They sit.
MEGAN comes back, crossing to BESSIE.)

MEGAN. Bessie, I've got incredible news.

BESSIE. You got yourself a show.

MEGAN. Yes!

BESSIE. So where is it? Off Broadway or Off Off?

MEGAN. Neither. It's a church in Brooklyn. What would you call that?

BESSIE. Out of town.... What's the show, girl? Tell me.

MEGAN. An old comedy. It's called "Arsenic and Old Lace."

BESSIE. Oh, dear Lord, my heart just stopped. That was my first show too.... You playing the ingénue?

MEGAN. Yes. What about you?

BESSIE. Same part. Only an all black cast.

MEGAN. Oh. Well we're mixed. White, black, Hispanic and Chinese.

BESSIE. Well, you're more liberal than we were.... I wish I could stay to see it.

MEGAN. Why can't you?

BESSIE. Leaving tomorrow night. I've gone Hollywood. A TV series. I sold my soul for more money than I'd make in ten years on the stage.

MEGAN. But won't you miss it?

BESSIE. I'm getting too old to have the luxury of missing things.

MEGAN. You won't miss any of it?

BESSIE. Oh, yes.... The ten seconds of joy.... Of stepping out, taking your bow and hearing the appreciation of an audience of real people.... Well, that's enough of that.... I'll see you before I go.

(BESSIE gets up and starts to go, passing MICKEY. MEGAN watches her, then turns back to work.)

MICKEY. Where are you going?

BESSIE. To Hollywood. To get rich.... You wanna come?

MICKEY. *(To ANDREW.)* So? What incredible project have you got for me this time?

ANDREW. Well, I'll be very candid with you, my friend. And you're going to be very surprised by this.... Would you consider coming to London for four months, to do a play in a ninety-seat theater for very little money?

MICKEY. *(Squints at ANDREW.)* My God. It sounds too good to toin down.

ANDREW. I'm not going to get my hopes up. It starts in September. I assume you're all booked.

MICKEY. Of course but who could say no for very little money for four months?... Tell me, if we get held over for another four months, do I get less money?

ANDREW. You must think me a complete ass to offer you this.

MICKEY. No. I thought of other parts of the anatomy too.... Listen, I don't always do something for money. Sometimes you have to do Art for Art's sake.... This sounds like an Art's Sake production.... You can't always just take. Sometimes you have to give.... And I'm glad you're doing Art for Art's Sake, for God's sake ... but I don't know....

ANDREW. Would you at least listen to me?

MICKEY. I'm listening.... But listening to you is like doing a benefit.... What is it?

ANDREW. A small masterpiece. I saw the most incredible play in Manchester, England. It got the most brilliant reviews but it's not for a popular audience. It won't go in a large London theater, but it could work very well in a small theater just outside of London proper.

MICKEY. *Outside* of London yet. The more you tell me, the more appealing it gets. I'm so lucky to get this offer. I'm assuming the part would have gone to Sir Laurence Olivier if he wasn't dead so long.

ANDREW. Actually it's only two scenes. You're on stage no more than twenty-five minutes.

MICKEY. This is good. This is very good. Because I've been looking everywhere for a play where I could sleep most of the evening.

ANDREW. I know you must think I'm out of my mind.

MICKEY. Andrew, you know me better than that. What do I play?

ANDREW. You would play a Jewish lawyer in a courtroom.

MICKEY. A Jewish lawyer, heh?... Do you think there's a Jewish lawyer in the woild who's only gonna talk for twenty-five minutes in a courtroom?

ANDREW. The role of the lawyer is not only uproariously funny, but rips your heart out with a riveting, explosive address to the jury. At the end of his speech, the applause has gone on and on and on.

MICKEY. Ninety seats just outside London, heh?... Of course I would insist that you put me up in a foist class four star bed and breakfast ... or is that not in the budget?...

ANDREW. Actually, the theater is adjacent to the river. And someone has agreed to put you up in their houseboat.

MICKEY. A houseboat, heh?... I could never sleep on a water-bed, how will I sleep in a houseboat?... Is it a private houseboat or does it take on sightseeing tours?

ANDREW. Am I crazy to ask you this, Mickey?

MICKEY. Stop it. I understand.

ANDREW. I swear to you, Mickey, this is an award-winning role. And there's so much more you can get out of this.

MICKEY. Like what? Like if my boat wins a race?

ANDREW. When I read the script, then saw the play, I thought, "My God, how magnificent Mickey would be in this."

MICKEY. But this sounds like serious theater.... I say to myself, am I up to this? Will I make a fool of myself?... Will the critics rip me apart?... Does the boat have a crew or do I pull up the anchor my-self?

ANDREW. There's no guarantees in the theater.

MICKEY. What about the guy who's playing it now?

ANDREW. He's good, not great. He doesn't have your style, your technique, your divine humor that is unique only to you.

MICKEY. Thank you. I'm afraid to ask where *he's* sleeping....

ANDREW. I think there's a deeper side to you that I sense intui-tively, something in you that's crying out to be heard.

MICKEY. Let me ask you a question.... How old is this lawyer?

ANDREW. It never really says. Why do you ask?

MICKEY. Instead of Mickey Fox, would you accept Steven Fox?

ANDREW. Who is Steven Fox?

MICKEY. My nephew.

ANDREW. *(Laughs.)* It's a joke. You're not serious.

MICKEY. You just asked me to woik for nothing in nowhere and sleep in a houseboat? I didn't laugh at you.

ANDREW. I'm sorry.

MICKEY. Then listen. I've been woiking with him for four months. At foist, I didn't think he had a chance. An amateur.... But now ... he suddenly blossomed. He's good. He talks like me, he thinks like me, he's been studying me for thirty years....

ANDREW. With all due respect, Mickey, I'm not looking for a mimic.

MICKEY. He's not. He took what I have and toined into what he can do. But if you think I can do this part, I think *he* can do it just as good.... Steven is the next me, as soon as I get through with me....

ANDREW. It's decent of you to look after his career, but he doesn't have your experience.

MICKEY. By next September he'll be close.... Do me a favor. No, do *yourself* a favor. Hear him. Audition him. Let him read the script for you.

ANDREW. Granted that he's good. I'd rather have you, Mickey.

MICKEY. Alright, here's the deal. I do it for four weeks. For no money. I'll sleep in my dressing room.... And if you like his audition, he plays the rest of the four months.

ANDREW. ... Oh, dear, Mickey. You have me over a barrel.

MICKEY. Please. I don't want to even picture what that looks like.... What do you say? I'll give him the script tonight.

ANDREW. Would you give me six weeks instead of four?

MICKEY. Would you give him a hotel room and he can ride the houseboat on Sundays?

ANDREW. ... You'd make a great agent, Mickey. Alright, tell me more about Steven....

(They lean in to talk. BERNIE comes out, pulls ZELDA aside to a quiet spot.

SOLOMAN enters from the lobby door. He doesn't look flush but he is wearing a light suit, probably made in Africa, and a white shirt, no tie. He sees BERNIE. Sneaks up behind him.)

SOLOMAN. Do you have any openings for a job?

BERNIE. *(Stops, doesn't turn.)* He's back. He's back to torture me. *(He turns, smiles.)* Soloman! I never expected to see you again. *(They embrace. SOLOMAN smiles.)* How are you?

SOLOMAN. Oh, very good. I must tell you, I made borscht for my friends—they got sick for three days.

(SOLOMAN laughs.)

BERNIE. Must be the beets.... What are you doing in New York?

SOLOMAN. I was invited by a friend. I was able to bring my wife along. She has family here. They wanted to see our newborn little boy.

BERNIE. You have a baby boy?

SOLOMAN. *(Nods.)* I named him Bernie. Bernie Mantutu.

BERNIE. Bernie Mantutu?... A Jewish Zulu?

SOLOMAN. Well, in Zulu it comes out Borwani.... But at home I call him Bernie because he too has a very generous nature. *(BERNIE hugs him again.)* ... Oh. There's Mr. Fox. I must go and say hello.

BERNIE. I'll go get Zelda.... Wait'll I tell her about Borwani.

(BERNIE goes.... SOLOMAN walks up behind MICKEY.)

SOLOMAN. You said you would write but I never *hoid* from you.

MICKEY. *(Turns quickly.)* Where were you? I told you to wait in the kitchen? *(He smiles.)* Come here. Gimme a hug. *(Then looks at him.)* You're looking cute, you know that?

SOLOMAN. Well, I'm very happy. I have a new son.

MICKEY. And I have a new nephew. We should get them together. They could play in the park.... You remember Andrew Duncan, don't you?

SOLOMAN. Indeed I do. Hello, Andrew.

MICKEY. How come you call him Andrew and you call me Mr. Fox?

SOLOMAN. Well, Andrew and I are working together. He saw

my play in Manchester and wants to produce it in London.... Haven't you told him yet, Andrew?

MICKEY. Your play??... It's YOUR PLAY??? ... You mean this whole thing was a plot? You came in here, ate soup you couldn't pay for, then got Bernie to hire you, you got friendly with me, talked me into reading your play so that one day I'd go to England and star in your play for very little money *outside* of London.

SOLOMAN. *(Laughs.)* No, of course not. Not at all.... It's not the starring role anyway.

MICKEY. *(To ANDREW.)* It's not even the starring role?

SOLOMAN. No. But it's the *best* role, by far.

ANDREW. *(To SOLOMAN.)* I've told him all about it. I just didn't ell him it was your idea to have him play it.

SOLOMAN. *(To MICKEY.)* Oh, don't misunderstand. I never dreamed you would actually do it. I just said to Andrew, "Wouldn't Mr. Fox be perfect in this play." And he said, "Let's call him." And I said, "Oh, no. He's a big star. And I wouldn't impose on him."

ANDREW. *(To MICKEY.)* And I said, "*I'll* impose on him. Let's fly to New York and ask him."

MICKEY. I see. So I toin down a major revival of "Fiddler on the Roof" to go outside London and do a twenty-five minute scene in a theater that has less seats than my mother has in her dining room.

SOLOMAN. No, of course not. I actually wanted to thank you for the advice you gave me. The play has been completely rewritten. I even got rid of the Zulu.... The only trouble I had was writing some humor into it.... So I thought, what if someone like Mr. Fox played the lawyer? And then it came to me so easily. That is you I put into those pages ... the way I heard and remembered you.... Of course I deepened the role and gave the man a conscience and a soul and a voice to my thoughts.... So you see, in a way you and I collaborated on it....

MICKEY. Listen, if I accidentally helped you, I'm very flattered. Did you leave in Horatio had fellatio?

SOLOMAN. No, but one bad night I was very tempted.

MICKEY. And now you have a son. What did you name him?

SOLOMAN. ... Bernie Mantutu.

MICKEY. *(Stares at him.)* No, seriously.
SOLOMAN. Seriously. Bernie Mickey Mantutu.
MICKEY. Really? That's the name they gave my uncle at Ellis Island.
SOLOMAN. And I understand why you couldn't possibly do the play.
MICKEY. I didn't say it was impossible.... You want Mr. Fox, I can get you Mr. Fox.
SOLOMAN. Do you mean it? You would actually do it?
ANDREW. It's a little more complicated than that, Soloman.
MICKEY. Instead of Mickey Fox, it's going to be Steven Fox.
SOLOMAN. Oh. If you wish to change your name, that is alright with me.
MICKEY. I'll tell you the truth, Soloman. I'm only going to play it for four weeks.... Then my nephew Steven Fox will take over.... If Andrew approves.
SOLOMAN. I approve.... To have you for four *days*, even for one day, is more than I ever hoped for. May I ask a question?
MICKEY. Yes.
SOLOMAN. Is he any good? I don't object to him playing it, but is he any good?
MICKEY. Trust me, Soloman. I wouldn't hurt you.
SOLOMAN. I know you wouldn't. But is he any good?
MICKEY. *(To ANDREW.)* See? He's talking like a playwright already.

(MICKEY puts one arm around SOLOMAN and hugs him. BERNIE and ZELDA come out of the kitchen.)

ZELDA. Soloman!... Oh, my God, it's so good to see you.

(They embrace.)

SOLOMAN. And you too, Zelda. I told my mother back home that I have another mother in New York.... And she was very happy.
ZELDA. That makes me feel so good.

SOLOMAN. And thanks to Andrew, I have another mother in London.

ZELDA. *(Less happy.)* Oh? Isn't that nice?

MICKEY. *(To SOLOMAN.)* And if you sell your play to the movies, wait'll you see the mothers in Hollywood. Whoo!

BERNIE. *(To SOLOMAN.)* I'm going to get you a plate of borscht.

ZELDA. Not you, Bernie. Sit with them. I like to see all my boys sitting together.

(ZELDA goes off as BERNIE joins them at the table. MEGAN comes out with a tray and sees SOLOMAN.)

MEGAN. Soloman Mantutu!

SOLOMAN. Megan Woods.... How is your acting coming?

MEGAN. I'm doing my first play. In a church in Brooklyn. What about you?

SOLOMAN. My play is already in Manchester, England. A small theater. Only seventy-five seats.

MICKEY. SEVENTY-FIVE SEATS??? *(To ANDREW.)* You told me ninety.... I want a bigger houseboat.... And a seaplane to get me to woik.

SOLOMAN. *(To MEGAN.)* I made you a promise.... Now I can keep it. *(He takes a thin paperback from his pocket, hands it to her.)* My play has been published.... I already signed it to you.

MEGAN. *(Takes the book.)* This is the absolute coolest thing I ever got. A first edition.... Thank you so much, Soloman.

SOLOMAN. And my wife and I also had a little boy.

MICKEY. Bernie Mickey Andrew Zelda Megan Mantutu ... the second.

MEGAN. That is fantastic.... Oh. My mother's coming in to see the play.

SOLOMAN. In Manchester?

MEGAN. In Brooklyn.

SOLOMAN. Oh. Of course.

(MEGAN goes off to deliver her tray.

SOLOMAN, MICKEY, BERNIE and ANDREW sit together and chat silently.
ARLEEN and CINDY have been listening to the previous conversations.)

CINDY. You mean the grapes were just a metaphor?
ARLEEN. Right.
CINDY. So why didn't they call it "My Father Was a Metaphor"?
ARLEEN. Not everyone knows what a metaphor is. Everyone knows what a grape is.

(The street door opens. CHARLES enters wearing his same gray suit but he looks more aware, more in control. With him is an older woman, dressed in a very plain dress and a short jacket. Her hair is gray and combed neatly. She walks with a cane, as if recuperating from an illness. No makeup on her. They both stand there.)
MEGAN crosses to them.)

MEGAN. Hello.
CHARLES. *(Speaks clearly.)* Just a table for two, please.
MEGAN. Anywhere in particular?
CHARLES. I think over there in the corner.... Is that alright with you, Rayleen?
RAYLEEN. *(With a much softer voice.)* Wherever you say, Charles. You know best. *(They walk to the table.)* Haven't we been here before, Charles?
CHARLES. Many times, dear. You've always like it.
RAYLEEN. Yes, I think I did.

(They sit. The men all look at them in wonderment.)

MEGAN. Would you like a tablecloth? I can get you one.
CHARLES. No. This is fine, thanks. *(MEGAN nods and leaves.)* Are you alright here, Rayleen?
RAYLEEN. Oh, yes.... Charles? Do I look alright?

CHARLES. You look wonderful, Rayleen.... Absolutely wonderful.

RAYLEEN. I do? Thank you, Charles. That's very sweet of you to say.

(RAYLEEN sits there looking at nothing in particular. CHARLES puts his hand on top of hers. The men have been watching this. Then SOLOMAN, BERNIE and ANDREW all look at MICKEY.)

MICKEY. Well, I'll tell you something.... Sometimes saying nothing is the poifect thing to say. *(The others agree with him.)* I can't believe we're going to lose this restaurant.... When does it go, Bernie?

BERNIE. I don't know. I got a letter today. I'm afraid to look. *(He takes out the letter and reads aloud.)* "My Dear Bernie, After thinking it over, I decided not to purchase the Polish Tea Room. I don't think anyone can run it as well as you and Zelda.... Thank you for the joy you've given me.... Most sincerely yours ... Charles W. Browning the third.

(BERNIE and ZELDA hug each other and MICKEY turns the other way and looks at CHARLES, who looks at MICKEY and smiles, then goes back to RAYLEEN.)

CURTAIN

Neil Simon began his writing career in television and established himself as our leading writer of comedy by creating a succession of Broadway hits beginning with *Come Blow Your Horn*. During the 1966-67 season, *Barefoot in the Park, The Odd Couple, Sweet Charity* and *The Star Spangled Girl* (stock rights only) were all running simultaneously; in the 1970-71 season, Broadway theatergoers had their choice of *Plaza Suite, Last of the Red Hot Lovers* and *Promises. Promises.*

Next carne *Little Me, The Gingerbread Lady, The Prisoner of Second Avenue, The Sunshine Boys, The Good Doctor, God's Favorite, They're Playing Our Song, I Ought to Be in Pictures, Fools,* a revival of *Little Me, Brighton Beach Memoirs, Biloxi Blues* (Tony Award) a new version of *The Odd Couple* starring Sally Struthers and Rita Moreno as the title duo, *Broadway Bound, Rumors, Lost in Yonkers* (Tony Award and Pulitzer Prize), *Jake's Women* and *London Suite.*

Mr. Simon has also written for the screen: the adaptations of *Barefoot in the Park, The Odd Couple, Plaza Suite, The Last of the Red Hot Lovers, The Prisoner of Second Avenue, The Sunshine Boys, California Suite, I Ought To Be In Pictures, Chapter Two, Brighton Beach Memoirs, Biloxi Blues,* the TV motion picture of *Broadway Bound* and *Lost in Yonkers.* Other screenplays he has written include *After the Fox, The Out-of-Towners, The Heartbreak Kid, Murder by Death, The Goodbye Girl, The Cheap Detective, Seems Like Old Times, Only When I Laugh, Max Dugan Returns* and *The Marrying Man.*

SKIN DEEP
Jon Lonoff

Comedy / 2m, 2f / Interior Unit Set

In *Skin Deep*, a large, lovable, lonely-heart, named Maureen Mulligan, gives romance one last shot on a blind-date with sweet awkward Joseph Spinelli; she's learned to pepper her speech with jokes to hide insecurities about her weight and appearance, while he's almost dangerously forthright, saying everything that comes to his mind. They both know they're perfect for each other, and in time they come to admit it.

They were set up on the date by Maureen's sister Sheila and her husband Squire, who are having problems of their own: Sheila undergoes a non-stop series of cosmetic surgeries to hang onto the attractive and much-desired Squire, who may or may not have long ago held designs on Maureen, who introduced him to Sheila. With Maureen particularly vulnerable to both hurting and being hurt, the time is ripe for all these unspoken issues to bubble to the surface.

"Warm-hearted comedy … the laughter was literally show-stopping. A winning play, with enough good-humored laughs and sentiment to keep you smiling from beginning to end."
– *TalkinBroadway.com*

"It's a little Paddy Chayefsky, a lot Neil Simon and a quick-witted, intelligent voyage into the not-so-tranquil seas of middle-aged love and dating. The dialogue is crackling and hilarious; the plot simple but well-turned; the characters endearing and quirky; and lurking beneath the merriment is so much heartache that you'll stand up and cheer when the unlikely couple makes it to the inevitable final clinch."
– *NYTheatreWorld.Com*

COCKEYED

William Missouri Downs

Comedy / 3m, 1f / Unit Set

Phil, an average nice guy, is madly in love with the beautiful Sophia. The only problem is that she's unaware of his existence. He tries to introduce himself but she looks right through him. When Phil discovers Sophia has a glass eye, he thinks that might be the problem, but soon realizes that she really can't see him. Perhaps he is caught in a philosophical hyperspace or dualistic reality or perhaps beautiful women are just unaware of nice guys. Armed only with a B.A. in philosophy, Phil sets out to prove his existence and win Sophia's heart. This fast moving farce is the winner of the HotCity Theatre's GreenHouse New Play Festival. The St. Louis Post-Dispatch called Cockeyed a clever romantic comedy, Talkin' Broadway called it "hilarious," while Playback Magazine said that it was "fresh and invigorating."

Winner!
of the HotCity Theatre GreenHouse New Play Festival

"Rocking with laughter...hilarious...polished and engaging work draws heavily on the age-old conventions of farce: improbable situations, exaggerated characters, amazing coincidences, absurd misunderstandings, people hiding in closets and barely missing each other as they run in and out of doors...full of comic momentum as Cockeyed hurtles toward its conclusion."

–Talkin' Broadway

TREASURE ISLAND
Ken Ludwig

All Groups / Adventure / 10m, 1f (doubling) / Areas

Based on the masterful adventure novel by Robert Louis Stevenson, *Treasure Island* is a stunning yarn of piracy on the tropical seas. It begins at an inn on the Devon coast of England in 1775 and quickly becomes an unforgettable tale of treachery and mayhem featuring a host of legendary swashbucklers including the dangerous Billy Bones (played unforgettably in the movies by Lionel Barrymore), the sinister two-timing Israel Hands, the brassy woman pirate Anne Bonney, and the hideous form of evil incarnate, Blind Pew. At the center of it all are Jim Hawkins, a 14-year-old boy who longs for adventure, and the infamous Long John Silver, who is a complex study of good and evil, perhaps the most famous hero-villain of all time. Silver is an unscrupulous buccaneer-rogue whose greedy quest for gold, coupled with his affection for Jim, cannot help but win the heart of every soul who has ever longed for romance, treasure and adventure.

THE OFFICE PLAYS

Two full length plays by Adam Bock

THE RECEPTIONIST

Comedy / 2m, 2f / Interior

At the start of a typical day in the Northeast Office, Beverly deals effortlessly with ringing phones and her colleague's romantic troubles. But the appearance of a charming rep from the Central Office disrupts the friendly routine. And as the true nature of the company's business becomes apparent, The Receptionist raises disquieting, provocative questions about the consequences of complicity with evil.

"...Mr. Bock's poisoned Post-it note of a play."
– *New York Times*

"Bock's intense initial focus on the routine goes to the heart of *The Receptionist's* pointed, painfully timely allegory... elliptical, provocative play..."
– *Time Out New York*

THE THUGS

Comedy / 2m, 6f / Interior

The Obie Award winning dark comedy about work, thunder and the mysterious things that are happening on the 9th floor of a big law firm. When a group of temps try to discover the secrets that lurk in the hidden crevices of their workplace, they realize they would rather believe in gossip and rumors than face dangerous realities.

"Bock starts you off giggling, but leaves you with a chill."
– *Time Out New York*

"... a delightfully paranoid little nightmare that is both more chillingly realistic and pointedly absurd than anything John Grisham ever dreamed up."
– *New York Times*

SAMUEL FRENCH STAFF

Nate Collins
President

Ken Dingledine
Director of Operations,
Vice President

Bruce Lazarus
Executive Director,
General Counsel

Rita Maté
Director of Finance

Accounting

Lori Thimsen | Director of Licensing Compliance
Nehal Kumar | Senior Accounting Associate
Josephine Messina | Accounts Payable
Helena Mezzina | Royalty Administration
Joe Garner | Royalty Administration
Jessica Zheng | Accounts Receivable
Andy Lian | Accounts Receivable
Zoe Qiu | Accounts Receivable
Charlie Sou | Accounting Associate
Joann Mannello | Orders Administrator

Business Affairs

Lysna Marzani | Director of Business Affairs
Kathryn McCumber | Business Administrator

Customer Service and Licensing

Brad Lohrenz | Director of Licensing Development
Fred Schnitzer | Business Development Manager
Laura Lindson | Licensing Services Manager
Kim Rogers | Professional Licensing Associate
Matthew Akers | Amateur Licensing Associate
Ashley Byrne | Amateur Licensing Associate
Glenn Halcomb | Amateur Licensing Associate
Derek Hassler | Amateur Licensing Associate
Jennifer Carter | Amateur Licensing Associate
Kelly McCready | Amateur Licensing Associate
Annette Storckman | Amateur Licensing Associate
Chris Lonstrup | Outgoing Information Specialist

Editorial and Publications

Amy Rose Marsh | Literary Manager
Ben Coleman | Editorial Associate
Gene Sweeney | Graphic Designer
David Geer | Publications Supervisor
Charlyn Brea | Publications Associate
Tyler Mullen | Publications Associate

Marketing

Abbie Van Nostrand | Director of Corporate Communications
Ryan Pointer | Marketing Manager
Courtney Kochuba | Marketing Associate

Operations

Joe Ferreira | Product Development Manager
Casey McLain | Operations Supervisor
Danielle Heckman | Office Coordinator, Reception

Samuel French Bookshop (Los Angeles)

Joyce Mehess | Bookstore Manager
Cory DeLair | Bookstore Buyer
Jennifer Palumbo | Customer Service Associate
Sonya Wallace | Bookstore Associate
Tim Coultas | Bookstore Associate
Monté Patterson | Bookstore Associate
Robin Hushbeck | Bookstore Associate
Alfred Contreras | Shipping & Receiving

London Office

Felicity Barks | Rights & Contracts Associate
Steve Blacker | Bookshop Associate
David Bray | Customer Services Associate
Zena Choi | Professional Licensing Associate
Robert Cooke | Assistant Buyer
Stephanie Dawson | Amateur Licensing Associate
Simon Ellison | Retail Sales Manager
Jason Felix | Royalty Administration
Susan Griffiths | Amateur Licensing Associate
Robert Hamilton | Amateur Licensing Associate
Lucy Hume | Publications Manager
Nasir Khan | Management Accountant
Simon Magniti | Royalty Administration
Louise Mappley | Amateur Licensing Associate
James Nicolau | Despatch Associate
Martin Phillips | Librarian
Zubayed Rahman | Despatch Associate
Steve Sanderson | Royalty Administration Supervisor
Douglas Schatz | Acting Executive Director
Roger Sheppard | I.T. Manager
Geoffrey Skinner | Company Accountant
Peter Smith | Amateur Licensing Associate
Garry Spratley | Customer Service Manager
David Webster | UK Operations Director

SamuelFrench.com
SamuelFrench-London.co.uk